DIG A LIT

'The ac

'There
America

Yorkshire Post

'Subtly menacing approach to an earthy mystery'

Express & Echo

DIG A LITTLE DEEPER

Ursula Curtiss

KEYHOLE CRIME
London · Sydney

First published in Great Britain 1976 by
Macmillan London Limited

This edition published 1982 by
Keyhole Crime, 15–16 Brook's Mews,
London W1A 1DR

ISBN 0 263 74028 5

The characters and situations in this book are entirely imaginary and bear no relation to any real person or actual happening.

06/0982

Made and printed in Great Britain by
Cox & Wyman Ltd., Reading

To my sister, Katherine Reilly

Chapter I

From the moment she reached the airport, Lydia Peel began to feel, or to imagine that she felt, a number of curious glances directed her way. They were not flattering glances, they were the glances of people who were wondering if a possible fellow passenger was carrying something with a ticking mechanism inside.

It was true that she was being extremely protective of the slender dark blue suitcase which was on-plane luggage, shielding it, sometimes even cradling it, from any close approach by other bags. But if she said, "It's a very old mirror," they would be all the more certain that there was a bomber in their midst. Fortunately there was no one who would have been expecting her to buy flight insurance; that would have been the finishing touch.

The mirror, to be delivered to Mrs. Emmett Blake in Elder's Farms, Connecticut, was a favor for Susan McGrath, a friend who owned the Santa Fe gallery adjoining the bookshop of which Lydia was part owner. Susan's sister Paula had moved with her husband from Boston to Elder's Farms a few months ago, and the mirror would be a combined birthday-housewarming present. Susan herself had an unconquerable fear of flying, and was afraid to trust such a breakable object to the mails. Would Lydia, as she was going to Elder's Farms anyway . . . ?

Lydia said yes, sympathetically; she had once investigated a resounding thump on her patio and found it to be a just-delivered package stamped Fragile in six places. Nevertheless, she worried about the mirror all the way to Connecticut—what if it was now, in spite of her care and its swaddling, a mass of quiet little shards? —and when her bride-to-be cousin Tracey Donahue met her at the station she said, observing the suitcase and Lydia's handling of it, "I see you've brought a few dozen eggs for the occasion."

At the house, full of flowers and light and the peculiar excitability of the night before a wedding, one of her cousins-in-law—they bore a remarkable resemblance to each other, like the Donahues, although they were unrelated—extended a friendly hand and said, "Here, let me take that for you," but Lydia clung to the case to the last. Upstairs, she opened it and took an anxious glance at her hazardous charge.

The mirror was Colonial. Its oval glass was intact within the frame of polished dark wood delicately rosetted at top and bottom. It showed her her own examining eyes, forward-swinging hair the color of well-done buttered toast, and nothing more. There were no shadows there at all.

It was ten years since Lydia had been in the house where she had spent her summers from the age of seven to sixteen. She had not then realized the increasing gravity of her father's illness, which turned her mother into an almost full-time nurse. Tom Donahue was her uncle, and as he and his wife Nancy had four daughters of their own, one more girl went almost unnoticed at a time of year which was spent largely at the beach.

The sameness of it, as with any background revisited from a distance of both time and personal events, was bemusing. Or perhaps that was partly physical: downstairs, holding a welcome drink, Lydia seemed to feel herself still humming with travel, as though the couch on which she sat had a forward propulsion.

What seemed an astonishing number of people had assembled in her absence upstairs, but they turned out to be only Tracey's three older sisters—all tall, vivid-eyed, dark-haired, bearing a hint of tan even in March—and their tall look-alike husbands. They were fast talkers, energetic, given to peals of laughter at obscure jokes and non-Donahues. This strong family feeling in an un-family age drew Lydia back into its comfortable spell. Tracey, sitting beside her, said contentedly, "It's marvelous the way we're so pleased with ourselves, but think how peaceful you'll be when we've all gone."

Because Tom and Nancy, following a tradition after their daughters' weddings, were departing for a week of recovery—Florida this time—and Lydia would occupy the house while they were away. Apart from her fondness for Tracey, who was closest to her in age and with whom she had shared the peculiar passions of adolescence, this was the chief reason why she had flown across the country. She had a decision to make, and Elder's Farms—as different from Santa Fe as it was possible to be—might give her perspective.

She had firmly declined to be a member of the wedding, on the grounds that it was too chancy a commitment at that remove of both time and space, and was horrified to discover that she was expected to attend the rehearsal dinner. "You *have* to," said Tracey, reproachful. "What would you do—hang around here and have a sandwich? Besides, we've asked a man for you. Desmond Moran; you might even remember him. He and Elizabeth had a thing going once."

Elizabeth was the oldest Donahue daughter. Lydia shook her head, but in her present state of fatigue old recognitions would not have come easily. The dinner went by her in a blur. Her partner, a man with a casual gray-eyed face, said, "Didn't I go up a tree after you once? It seems to me . . . Never mind," he was kind about it, "I think you're asleep."

This roused Lydia temporarily, and she said to Tom Donahue at the first opportunity, "Would you happen to know the Emmett Blakes? They moved here right after Christmas, I think, and they live on Violet Lane. He inherited the place from a relative, Simon something. That's who the mirror is for."

The Donahues communed among themselves and said no. "I've met them," said Lydia's dinner partner surprisingly. "They live near me."

She waited for the usual follow-up of "They seem pleasant," or even "They seem unpleasant," and while she waited she had a flashing memory, buried until now, of being high up in a pine tree on a dare, panicking, feeling a competent hand close over her ankle and hearing a calm voice say, "There's a good branch under you, you can feel it with your toes if you reach." That had been the summer of the frightful khaki-colored shorts, which didn't fit.

The same hand was now reaching out to an ash tray, and its owner was engrossed in putting out his cigarette. It did not occur to Lydia until later that he had given this small action the attention of a man extinguishing a campfire in tinder-dry woods.

By four-thirty the next afternoon she was alone in the house.

A cleaning woman had arrived as they were leaving for the church, and now only the flowers on end tables and mantel remained as festive echoes of the wedding. Tracey, almost unrecognizable in white slipper satin with her hair piled high, had wept a little going down the aisle on her father's arm. Coming back from the reception, Lydia had made a slow circuit of the familiar grounds for the pure pleasure of being out in the moist and darkening air; soon, probably, she would begin to think wistfully of the New Mexico sun, but for the moment she felt like an amphibious creature returned to its other element.

The house, white clapboard with bluish-green shutters faded to the color of old silk, was over a hundred and fifty years old. It occupied only an acre a few miles outside the town, but this had never mattered to the growing children, as there was a pond for skating across the road and the beach was only a ten-minute drive away. Inside, its woodwork was snowy, its black-latched doors paneled in the traditional cross, its lower windows scraped, when the wind blew, by lilacs and honeysuckle. Lydia saw that the long mirror over the dining-room fireplace still held a precise leaf-shaped crack, the result of her having placed a candle too close to it one summer night when a storm had knocked out the electricity. "Lydia Peel: her mark," Tracey had observed yesterday.

. . . The other mirror, suitcased upstairs. Gift of Susan

McGrath to her sister; Susan who, four years after the death of her husband in a horrifying and needless highway accident, had fallen violently in love again. The man was good-looking in a distinguished way, charming, devoted, and a thief.

An iron-grilled glass door between the bookshop and the gallery was propped wide during business hours, and twice, in its reflection, Lydia had seen Miles Marsh casually pocket smallish objects—a Durer print the first time, and then a piece of primitive stone sculpture. On both occasions he was alone in the gallery, waiting for the arrival of an assistant while Susan got ready to go to lunch with him.

Tell her? Susan had inched herself back from a nervous breakdown like a woman clawing for handholds on an apparently smooth mountain face. Not tell her, in view of probable marriage, and be faced eventually with "You must have guessed, being right next door. You must have had an inkling"?

Was it even possible that Susan had guessed, and in the depths of her infatuation didn't care? In that case she would be bitter indeed at shared knowledge.

Lydia had gone as far as she dared, obliquely, saying when Susan was mourning the loss of the sculpture, "It was there at twelve-thirty, I know, because I wandered in and couldn't resist picking it up—it's like holding a nice warm egg. You must have been there after I left, Miles—did a customer come in?"

Eyes meeting eyes: either he saw no trap or he was utterly confident of Susan. He raised a forefinger in a concentrating way. "Wait—you're right. A woman tourist, with one of those gigantic bags they carry. She must have had an eye on it, because she was in and out in about thirty seconds."

But, although Susan said resignedly that shoplifting was a growing problem everywhere, there had been no woman, no customer of either sex.

Maybe, in an indirect fashion, consult Paula Blake? Lydia knew that the sisters were close in spite of their geographical separation; they exchanged long letters at least once a month. Susan had her mail delivered at the gallery and sometimes, sharing midmorning coffee, burst out laughing at something in the closely typed sheets of yellow copy paper from Paula.

A wind stole suddenly off the dim silver ice of the pond across the road, and Lydia shivered and went back into the house.

Presently, at the telephone on top of the dining-room bookcase, directory assistance informed her that there was no listing for an Emmett Blake at 12 Violet Lane or anywhere else. Choice, or a waiting list? Lydia suspected choice; Susan had said that her sister and brother-in-law, surprised at an inheritance they hadn't expected so soon, had impulsively given up their jobs in Boston and were allowing themselves an experimental year in Elder's Farms, Emmett to paint, Paula to try a book instead of advertising copy. It was not the kind of atmosphere in which they would want friends calling up in the hope of being invited for country weekends.

They would also, Lydia suspected, not welcome any intrusion during working hours, which, from a few similarly occupied friends in Santa Fe, she took to be morning. She waited until three o'clock before, the next day, she placed the suitcased mirror carefully on the seat of the Donahues' oldish blue Volvo and set out for Violet Lane.

Chapter 2

Although Elder's Farms had been largely by-passed by the New York advertising community in favor of its parent town of Elder, there were changes enough to make Lydia lose her way twice. A new bridge had been put in over the river, and an enormous field dominated by three oaks at its farther end, which she had counted on as a reference point, had become a housing development.

But it was a day to drive for the pleasure of driving. New Mexico might have been on another continent. This sky was a windy seethe of asphalt-undersided white clouds, with pieces of tender blue appearing occasionally like something being boiled in a vast pot. After dizzy gold mountain-hung distances, the woods and hills seemed close enough to touch, the architecture, in contrast to the fluid, cornerless molding of adobe, spare and precise.

Violet Lane was a narrow, curving dead-end road, and it took a persevering eye to find the break in a wall of lilacs which harbored No. 12. The driveway wound down past a knoll whose crown was flattened curiously, then curled to the left. The house, a weathered saltbox with apple trees beside and behind it, appeared with the effect of a rush.

The Blakes were evidently at home; there was a dark green Austin Marina, very splashed and muddy, parked in front. Lydia put the Volvo beside it, walked around the car and took out the suitcase, slamming both doors with a great and premonitory loudness. Paula Blake would certainly have had Susan's covering letter by now; still, arriving anywhere without having telephoned first made her sharply uncomfortable. She had mounted the single stone step to the front door and was reaching for the knocker when, just on the other side of the door—or was there a flanking window a little open even on this cold day?—a man's voice, low and explosive, said, "Christ, what now?"

Instantly, soundlessly, Lydia deposited the suitcase on the step (like an unwanted baby, went wildly through her mind) and was halfway to the car when the door opened and a woman's voice called after a moment for comprehension, "Hello—you must be Lydia Peel. Come on in, won't you?"

"Thanks, but I really have to be getting back," said Lydia pleasantly. "I just wanted to deliver the mirror while it was still in one piece."

"You heard my husband," said Paula Blake ruefully, pulling the door to behind her and coming down the step. She wasn't as tall as Susan and she was compact rather than slight. She wore dark blue slacks and a loose cream pullover, and hugged herself against the wind. Her light green eyes behind shell-rimmed glasses looked genuinely distressed. "I'll explain later, but *please* come in. I'll never forgive myself or Emmett if you don't, and Susan will never forgive either of us."

It was impossible to refuse without giving an impression of iron pique. Stiff with reluctance, all her fears come true about unheralded arrivals, Lydia followed her inside and into a low-windowed living room painted—very recently, from the smell—Wedgwood blue and white. Combined with the patches of brilliance still roiling about in the sky, the very air seemed blue.

There was a fire burning in the fireplace—"This place is the devil to heat," said Paula—and on one side of it stood Emmett Blake, a tall, mid-fortyish man with a seasoned-looking face and, by contrast, the smooth fair hair of a choirboy. He greeted Lydia without a trace of embarrassment, giving her a conspiratorial wink as he introduced the woman who occupied, in a four-square way, an antique chair on the other side of the hearth. "This is Mrs. Chilton, a neighbor of ours. She's an old hand in these parts and has very kindly been steering us away from the local pirates."

Was this woman the focal point of the previous tension? If so, she seemed unaware of it, addressing herself cordially to Lydia in an English-accented voice, leaning forward with her gray head cocked, her disarming beaky-nosed face alight with interest, to admire the mirror which Paula produced from the suitcase. During this process she dislodged a spark from her cigarette; almost at once, an acrid smell of burning began to issue from her tweed lap.

Paula and Emmett Blake watched tranquilly; it was left to Lydia to say involuntarily, "Mrs. Chilton, your skirt!"

"Oh, damnation," said Mrs. Chilton, brushing good-humoredly at her lap. "I have holes in everything I own. Why doesn't the Surgeon General speak up about this, may I ask?"

The Blakes laughed, and the mirror was held tentatively against one wall and then another. For Lydia, remembering the fury in Emmett's voice only a few minutes earlier, the scene had an almost surrealist air: it was like hearing an unmistakable crash of glass in the next room, and stepping in to find that there wasn't a single splinter on the floor.

Decisively, after what she obviously judged to be a graceful interval, Mrs. Chilton heaved herself forward and up out of her chair, said brisk good-byes, and was eased by Emmett into a capacious beige raincoat. She hadn't exaggerated about her wardrobe, apparently; the coat had three burnt holes in a triangle under one pocket, giving her the aspect of having been shot at by an inexpert marksman. And yet, thought Lydia, in spite of the holes and the short undisciplined hair and the sturdy round-toed walking shoes, there was nothing ridiculous or even countrified about Mrs. Chilton; she had, instead, an air of having willingly abdicated a command elsewhere and being amused at her new circumstances.

"—oh, and, Mr. Blake," she was saying as Emmett conducted her in the direction of the door, "do think, won't you, about what we've been discussing? Your cousin Simon did agree, I assure you."

"I will," said Emmett's diminishing voice, "when—" and Lydia lost the rest of that because Paula, plunging her fingers into her dark copper hair and giving it a backward flip, was saying cautiously, "Well, thank God for *that.* I thought she was going to take root."

Lydia schooled her face to polite inquiry. She had liked Mrs. Chilton; she wasn't at all sure she liked either of the Blakes.

"She's nice enough in a way," said Paula, still in an attitude of guarded listening, "but she seems to think that having been a crony of Simon Wister's—or do you suppose crony is the masculine of crone?—gives her the right to pester Emmett about buying some of the furniture here. Simon must have made her some vague promises, so we've already parted with a nice old carved chest from the hall, but it's really a bit of a trial. Why she should want antiques at all is beyond me, as her house is all contemporary. Nothing creaks," said Paula with a certain crisp envy, "and everything works."

("Something tells me," Susan had remarked after getting her sister's most recent letter, "that Paula isn't finding life in the country all it's cracked up to be.")

"I suppose that's the point of wills," murmured Lydia for no better reason than that Paula seemed to be watching her expectantly, and Emmett came back in, bringing a curl of cold air with him. "I tried to drive her home," he said, clearly addressing Paula but gazing at Lydia, "but she insisted the walk would be good for what she calls her figger. Why are we not having a drink?"

Lydia protested—it would soon be dusk and she didn't want to lose her way going home—but was prevailed upon to accept one. Paula turned on lamps, established herself on the couch with a cigarette, and came at once to the point. "I think it's marvelous about this new man of Susan's. She adored Bill, but four years isn't exactly the twinkling of an eye and she had such a ghastly time. Would you guess marriage was in the wind? What's Miles like?"

At some point, Lydia's mind had made itself up. To expose Miles Marsh to these casual but sure people, even if they were Susan's younger sister and brother-in-law, would be to expose Susan, and even a good friend had no authority for that. She had a feeling, not pleasant, that they would be like expert dogs let off leashes. She said, "Very nice. Intelligent, quite attractive."

"What does he do?" That was Emmett, idle.

Thrust out of her mind the single word that came into her head. "He's with a public-relations firm, I think. Something like that." Lydia stood, firmly. "I got lost twice on the way here, in broad daylight, so I really must take off. It's so very nice to have—"

This time the protest was the Blakes'. They had scarcely had a chance to talk to her, what with Mrs. Chilton; they hadn't even thanked her properly for portaging the mirror; she must have dinner with them before she went back to Santa Fe. Paula would call and find out what night was convenient.

Perhaps because of the lamplight combined with the cocktail, the blue and white room looked serene and charming, and the Blakes—with Lydia's nerve-end prickliness restored to its proper context of reaction to the long flight, the total change of climate, the carried-over fatigue from everything that surrounded the wedding—were attractive, civilized people who had had to struggle out of an initial awkwardness. They had not been secretly entertained at an elderly woman's nearly setting her skirt on fire; they had simply warned or reminded her so often that they were resigned. Lydia gave Paula the Donahues' address and telephone number, waved to their silhouetted figures in the doorway, and drove off.

It was not quite dusk, but the woods had thickened as though darkness might come swarming out of them at any moment. Lydia fumbled around the unfamiliar dashboard, surprised herself with windshield wipers and jetting water, located the headlight switch and pulled it on. Almost at once, although she was less than a quarter of a mile from the Blakes' house, the beams picked up the stoutly trudging figure of Mrs. Chilton.

Paula Blake finished her drink at a gulp and held out her empty glass. "Did you really offer Mrs. Chilton a ride home?"

"I certainly did, and when she refused I saw her safely off the premises. We chatted of this and that," said Emmett, taking the glass. "How did you get on with our visitor?"

"Oh, swimmingly. She's quite attractive, isn't she? I didn't really expect boots and a big hat, but I thought she might be draped all over in Indian jewelry." Paula's gaze—she had removed her glasses and without them she looked younger and much less sure of herself—turned pensive. "Did you get the impression that she didn't want to say much about Miles Marsh?"

Emmett nodded. "That's why I thought dinner was a good idea."

He went out to the kitchen, made drinks, returned to find Paula studying herself in the small Colonial mirror. "You know what this means, don't you?" she asked. "Now I'm going to have to start looking around for Susan's birthday."

"Yes, I know. Last year," Emmett's face took on an air of concentration, "I seem to remember you hunting down a pair of chichi sunglasses . . ."

"And," said Paula as if she hadn't heard, "if we're going to make a success of this venture at all, we're going to have to do something quite firm about droppers-in. Like Mrs. Chilton."

Softly, after a few minutes, Emmett began to whistle,

not tunelessly but with definition. In spite of this particular arrangement of notes, the lamplight did not dim or waver, and to anyone looking through a window the blue and white room would not have lost an iota of its tranquil charm.

Chapter 3

"How very kind of you!" said Mrs. Chilton, settling herself into the Volvo with a gusty sigh of relief. She propped a formidable walking stick between her lisle-clad knees and answered the question which had wandered into Lydia's mind. "Normally I have my car, but my daughter is visiting me with her little boy and she likes to get out now and then. If you turn right at the top of this hill, it's only about a mile . . . How do you like Elder's Farms? I imagine it's very different from the Southwest?"

Lydia explained about the summers here, and Mrs. Chilton seemed captivated by this evidence of taste and judgment. "Now the Blakes were *quite* strangers when they first came. I remember Mr. Blake visiting his cousin years ago, but that was only for a week or so and it hardly counts, and Mrs. Blake seems quite—urban."

"His cousin must have been very taken with him," remarked Lydia, by-passing the last of that and negotiating a curve with care.

"Oh, Simon Wister was a very family-minded man. It would never have occurred to him to leave so much as a stick or a stone elsewhere. He died of a heart attack playing golf one day," added Mrs. Chilton reminiscently, "although he'd had a warning or two before. Everybody said wasn't it nice that he went that way." She uttered a sound closely resembling a snort. "Actually, I've never been able to see that point of view. I'd much rather go when I was facing something I loathe, like cleaning out the refrigerator. Mine's the next driveway on the right."

The headlights picked it out a moment later, just beyond a grove of birches leaning tipsily behind a gray stone wall. Lydia realized with surprise that she had driven a long narrow U; if it had not been for a wooded hill in between, she would probably have been able to see the lights at the Blakes'. The shape of the house at the end of the driveway was long and low against the remnants of smoked silver in the west. One big window was lit; presumably the daughter was at home.

". . . must have marvelous digs in New Mexico," Mrs. Chilton was saying enviously, and Lydia, led astray by the context of her own thoughts and the briskly accented voice, had to blink mentally until memory supplied what had gone before. She said yes, that there had been some important archeological discoveries even within the last few years, and—in answer to a further question—that her own activities in this area had been limited to walking along arroyos after an occasional rain or an exceptionally high wind.

"And what d'you find?" Perhaps because the dashboard glow threw her expectantly turned face into a new pattern of light and shadow, Mrs. Chilton looked as eager and hopeful as a child. Could she possibly, in spite of her eminently sensible appearance, be thinking in terms of gold or other treasure?

"Oh . . . bits of Indian pottery, petrified wood, shaped stones sometimes—nothing valuable, but it's fun looking," said Lydia, and drew to a halt beside a big dark old-fashioned car parked before the front door.

"Simon once found part of a pewter plate." With renewed thanks, Mrs. Chilton negotiated herself and her stick out of the Volvo, and bent in again to say—a trifle dubiously?—"Won't you come in and meet my daughter Candide?"

Something in Lydia's midriff leaped like a startled fish. She said, "I think I'd better be getting home," and Mrs. Chilton withdrew, saying with an unmistakable element of relief, "Perhaps I'll see you again before you leave."

Good nights, waves; Lydia backed and turned. In her rear-view mirror, the door which had closed upon Mrs. Chilton opened again and a man emerged. In the fractional second before he swung around to complete his farewells, he was clearly identifiable as Lydia's partner at the rehearsal dinner.

It was after five-thirty when she reached the Donahue house; with lighted windows springing out of what by daylight had seemed to be untenanted woods and emptily folded hills, it was as though a whole new map had been superimposed on the old. She hadn't thought, at three o'clock, to leave a lamp burning, and as she used her key, she reflected uneasily that that hadn't been very wise. Anyone who read the local paper, which meant virtually the entire town, would know that there had just been a wedding in the family, and although the departure of the Donahues hadn't been mentioned, the Volvo had been gone since midafternoon.

But the darkness inside was faintly flower-scented and totally innocent; there was no suggestion of checked whispers or arrested movements. Still, when she had switched on lights, Lydia went up the stairway against the far living-room wall, her legs still a little surprised at this activity after ten years of living on one level, and, in the Donahues' big corner bedroom, tested the door of the closet that held a large collection of wedding presents. ("We don't want you to feel like a security guard.") It remained firmly locked.

Downstairs in the kitchen, which had been built when kitchens were used for more than cooking and ran the whole width of the house, Lydia made herself a drink and inspected the icebox. A healthy portion of roast beef and almost half a turkey remained. She found and sliced tomatoes for grilling, turned on the eye-level oven next to the old black iron range, cast an affectionate eye at the round oak table, scarred but imperishable, where she and Tracey had occupied themselves on innumerable rainy days, and carried her drink back to the living room and the six o'clock news.

The pond across the road glimmered watchfully back at her, and she drew the moss-green velvet curtains. She watched and heard but did not absorb the news. The slight fragrance of roses and carnations and, presently, grilled tomatoes, was replaced by the salty smell of wet bathing suits, damp wood, sizzling hot dogs . . .

. . . She was sixteen that final year before the move to the Southwest for her father's health, and irrevocably in love with Kewpie Blythe, a summer visitor like herself, a tall, faun-faced seventeen-year-old boy whom most of the beach watched when he executed his airy, floating swan dives, his nimble double back flips. For his sake Lydia had disloyally deserted the first float, immemorial goal of her cousins, for the second float a hundred yards away; for his sake, hair tied back with a pink ribbon instead of a grim bathing cap, she had said nonchalantly, "Tell me what I'm doing wrong, will you?" and plunged herself in utter terror from the diving board.

In her inexperience, she dove too deep. The heavy chain that anchored the float grazed her cheek, the hard rippled gold sand held the memory of a classmate of Tracey's who had caught a finger inextricably in the chain and drowned the summer before. She pushed frantically with her legs and broke the surface, scraped and gasping, to find Kewpie Blythe treading water and holding out a hand. "Don't *scare* me like that," he said, and they swam slowly and companionably back to shore.

"You need a few diving lessons, like maybe fifty," Kewpie told her, and held her hand protectively while they walked along the hollowly echoing boardwalk to the pavilion. There were the usual bench sitters and commentators on the way, and "Look at me," sang Lydia soundlessly, "I'm walking along with Kewpie Blythe!"

The pavilion, with its griddles and Coca-Cola dispensers and juke-box and splintery uneven tables, was, if you were with an enviable boy, a kind of Stork Club for the young. Status was acquired here. Eyes rolled eloquently or dropped in winks, heads came together, whispers started. Although she kept her lashes demurely down, Lydia's body buzzed with love and excitement when Kewpie Blythe came masterfully back with two Cokes, gave her a deep look from under peaked brows, said, "Where you from?"

"New Roch—"

But, with thunderclap suddenness, Kewpie Blythe no longer cared where she came from or where she went; he had shot to his feet and said "Hi" in a casual tone completely undone by his enveloping blush. Lydia swiveled, and there behind her in a pale pink linen shift was Candide Chilton.

Candide was nineteen, and an object of considerable awe in Elder's Farms. Not only did she speak with an English accent, she had just come back from a year abroad. She had ash-blonde hair knotted on top of her head with an effect of carelessness, bisque skin, slate-colored eyes, and the general appearance of an insolent Madonna. People who wanted to curry favor said she was shy; right-thinking people said she was arrogant. Lydia, so heart-poundingly happy a second ago, felt like a wet rat in her bathing suit; even the dried sand on the soles of her feet seemed to crunch out loud.

The slaty glance touched her briefly, the corners of the sculptured mouth moved microscopically downward in what was Candide's smile. She said drawlingly to Kewpie, "Someone told me you were good with cars. Would you have a try at starting mine?"

Kewpie Blythe didn't tell Lydia he would be right back, or instruct her to mind his Coke. He simply uttered a distracted "See you" which was if anything more dismissive than "Good-bye forever," and left with Candide Chilton at such speed that he bumped the table in passing.

It seemed logical to believe that she was the cynosure of all eyes. Lydia sipped carelessly at her Coke, which settled into her stomach like a trayful of ice cubes, gazed interestedly into the middle distance as though something pleasant had just crossed her mind, and left the pavilion with majestic unconcern. It was fortunate for her composure that, with her deeper wounds, she had forgotten her blazing and bloodied cheek.

. . . Lydia became aware that she was gazing at a headache-remedy commercial in which a great gong was being beaten inside a cut-away woman's head; the woman wore an expression of pained reproach which hardly seemed equal to the occasion. She sprang up hastily, switched off the set before her own head could absorb any more of this message, went out to the kitchen to inspect her tomatoes.

Candide Chilton wasn't wearing pink tonight, she thought irrelevantly; there had been a flash of warm red in the doorway. Strange that she had made no connection at all when Emmett Blake introduced her to Mrs. Chilton—but she had still tingled from the reaction to her arrival, in ten years she had heard other English accents, there was no faintest resemblance between mother and daughter.

In the dining room the telephone rang, startling as always in the quiet house. Lydia answered it, automatically preparing to add a message to the two for the Donahues the evening before, and a man said, "Lydia Peel."

For some reason she knew his voice at once, although she had never registered his name and remembered only his amused and sympathetic gaze while she was trying to look like a living person during the rehearsal dinner.

"This is Desmond Moran. I have your cigarette lighter; you left it on the table the other night. I'm in town and I could drop it off in about five minutes if I wouldn't be interrupting anything."

Lydia said not at all and that would be very kind, turned off her grilled tomatoes and—reflex action from the sharp memory of dripping hair, damp bathing suit, sandy bare feet?—used lipstick and comb in what had been an enormous closet her last summer here and was now the downstairs bath. She had missed if not actually mourned the lighter; ever since losing a Christmas-present Dunhill she had stuck to the disposable kind.

Desmond Moran, she found herself thinking a few minutes later, did not look remotely like Kewpie Blythe except for his eyes, which were as intensely clear as if he had just been swimming. "I would have had this back to you sooner but I had to go to Forest Hills and be a godfather," he said. "How did things go off?"

Perhaps because the afternoon had been so peculiarly bemusing that the white satin and champagne and electric gaiety seemed pushed back to a false point in time, it took Lydia seconds to realize that he meant the wedding. "Not a hitch. Tracey looked beautiful," she said, and then, because she could not simply stand there gazing at him and he was after all a good friend of the Donahues', "Can I offer you a drink?"

She could. Seated with it, his coat slung unceremoniously over the other end of the couch with a gesture suggesting that this was his firm way with all coats, Desmond Moran said in answer to her polite inquiry that the godchild in question was a new niece so bald that she made an egg look hairy, but that if she ever did acquire hair it would probably be much the color of Lydia's. Without transition, he added, "I see that you found your friends, the Blakes."

Mrs. Chilton would have responded to her daughter's probable query as to who had driven her home; of course. "Yes, I did," said Lydia, letting the appellation go uncorrected because it was too much bother to explain. She reached for a cigarette and Desmond Moran snapped on her own lighter for her: "There. Your first cigarette in forty-eight hours . . . I understand that the Blakes had been living in Boston before they moved here, but you know"—he was back on the couch again, arm stretched along the back, relaxed and confiding—"I could swear I saw Mrs. Blake in New Orleans three years ago."

Lydia regarded him in wonderment. "People do take trips. Especially from Boston."

"I know. I mentioned it to Mrs. Blake and she said New Orleans was a place she'd always wanted to see but never had. Oh, well . . ." He shrugged as though losing interest but he could not very well shrug his watchful eyes. "Has she a sister?"

"Yes, she has—" Lydia began, and stopped herself right there. If Desmond Moran really had met Paula Blake in New Orleans, and for some reason Paula wanted to deny it, who was Lydia to tell him that no one could possibly mistake Susan McGrath for her sister? She gazed uncommunicatively back at the man on the couch, and the sound of the telephone broke off what was almost a tug of war.

"May I speak to Miss Lydia Peel, please?" A woman's voice, light, crisp, faintly commanding, conveying the impression that in the houses she called the telephone was answered by minions.

"This is Lydia. Hello, Candide."

"Lydia! How remarkable of you to recognize my voice after such eons. Mother told me you were in town and in fact you'd given her a lift home." Well, at least she had stopped saying Mummy. "We must get together while you're here—what about tomorrow, now that I have you on the phone?"

Lydia considered saying that she was tied up until plane time, but gave in to the curiosity that always wants to know what ten years have done to another female, and a heartily disliked one at that. Still, she made it four o'clock, so that Candide would have to hurry home and feed her child.

"Oh, and might I bring a friend?" Hard to believe: the assured tones sounded a trifle arch.

The child, outwitting that plan? Lydia said certainly, and thought that the conversation had drawn to its natural end except for mutual statements that they would be looking forward. This was not the case. "Is Desmond Moran there, by any chance?" inquired Candide.

How was it possible to feel instantly like a bartender? "Yes, he is. Hold on," said Lydia briefly, and laid the receiver down on the bookcase. "For you," she said in the living-room doorway. "Candide Chilton."

"Candide Blackwood," corrected Desmond Moran. "I mentioned that I might be returning your lighter." Lydia, continuing on into the living room and lighting a cigarette too soon after the last, heard him say, "Yes . . . No, no trouble at all . . . About half an hour, I'd say."

The receiver was replaced and he came back and shouldered his way into his coat. "She has a boy about four," he said conversationally at the door. "A capital little fellow—you should hear him play the piano. Thanks for the drink, I'll return it if I may."

Lydia's grilled tomatoes, which hadn't been quite done when she turned off the oven, had now settled into wretched little huddles. She sliced roast beef thin, located horseradish, and ate her dinner in the dining room which, with its fireplace and Dutch oven and long mirror and black-latched door enclosing a stairway that paralleled the open one in the living room, was her favorite spot in the house. She tidied the kitchen, read for a long time, carried her book up to bed.

The night before, when she was falling asleep, the problem of Susan McGrath—tell her about Miles or not?—had loomed in her mind like a coatrack in an otherwise empty room. Tonight, because of small elusive things that had been said during the infinitely long day, the coatrack was replaced by a shadow that, for the moment, was content to occupy a corner.

At one point she woke to a sound of menace but, although she had never been here in late winter before, realized that the temperature must have dropped sharply and it was only a hollow and icy quake from the pond across the road.

Chapter 4

In his rented apartment at the back of the Chilton property, Desmond Moran lay awake a good deal longer than Lydia Peel. He was like a man with a mental splinter. It could not be ignored, would not go away by itself, and must therefore be removed.

He was one of the twelve people, out of a passenger list of seventy-two, who had walked away—or, more accurately, been carried—from a plane crash in Atlanta two months earlier. His fractured shoulder and collarbone mended, his leg burns healed, he had still had to cope with the things seen and heard immediately after impact. A report filed from the hospital even before he went into surgery was only a partial catharsis. The newspaper on which he worked had given him sick leave, and when he emerged from the hospital, he had looked at the streets of Manhattan, with the micromobs drifting suggestively together on street corners, the harried faces fleeing into and out of subways, the mindless get-out-of-my-way pace, and thought that there must be a better place to finish his other healing.

He had been to college with and still frequently saw Kevin Howard, now an executive in a publishing house; with Kevin, who as a senior was already determined to marry Joan Donahue, he had journeyed down to Elder's Farms for numerous weekends. For a time he had gone about concentratedly with Joan's older sister Elizabeth, but a point arrived when their attitudes toward each other took on the almost audible tick of cooling metal. They liked each other very much and that was all.

Elder's Farms, probably because of those unworried days, had beckoned like an oasis. Kevin Howard had said confidently, "Tom and Nancy will find you a place," and they had.

The apartment had been built by Edward Chilton, a photographer specializing in children's portraits, as a combination studio, darkroom and office. A mercurial man, he occasionally refused young subjects after studying them, and "Portrait by Chilton" became a mark of status as a result. He made a great deal of money but considered a month in Europe twice a year one of the bare necessities of life, and upon his death it became clear that Mrs. Chilton would have to augment her income. The reconverted studio-darkroom-office had had a number of tenants before Desmond, mostly in the summer, and he sometimes entertained himself with explanations for the large brown crock of hickory nut shells which stood with an air of permanence in a corner of his living room. Someone had been planning to do nutshell paintings—souvenir of the woods instead of the beach—or sabotage an enemy's Grape-Nuts, or play practical jokes on squirrels.

Purely out of habit, and as his own private rites of exorcism, he had begun to peck away at his typewriter. What he at first conceived as a short story about a plane crash did not want to end there; it stretched out of its own volition. In the mornings he worked, in the afternoons he walked and, two or three times a week, drove into the town for supplies. On a snowy day in late February he had armed himself with milk and was reaching for coffee in Elder's Farms' one supermarket when a woman's voice said in a rapid mutter, "Quick, let's get out of here, there comes that old horror."

For a fleeting and outraged moment Desmond thought that this unhandsome epithet referred to him; then he turned his head and saw approaching from the far end of the aisle the stout and energetic form of Mrs. Chilton. He was not much mollified; he liked Mrs. Chilton and was prepared instantly to dislike the speaker. He glanced back as he moved away with his coffee, and she looked over her shoulder at the same time as though suddenly aware that she might have been overheard. Not tall, early or mid-thirties, light green eyes behind shell-rimmed glasses, side-parted red-brown hair, perhaps overridingly an air of total assurance. She clicked into his memory as exactly as a photograph being slid into its frame.

New Orleans. He couldn't remember having been introduced to her, but he had all he needed for the special-interest Mardi Gras piece he was there for and neither he nor the colleague he was with that evening was entirely sober. Afterwards he had equated her in terms of—some kind of unpleasantness, accusation?

A week later, at the public library, Mrs. Chilton had introduced her and the fair-haired man with her as Paula and Emmett Blake. That was when Desmond had said, "We met three years ago, I think, in New Orleans. At the Mardi Gras. I have to confess that I'm a little vague about the circumstances."

She had smiled ruefully. "I'm afraid not." The light green gaze was open and unwavering. "New Orleans is a place I'd love to see and never have."

When the Blakes had left, Mrs. Chilton was thoughtful and perplexed. "Simon Wister and I were friends for twenty years, and I'd hoped—my house *is* a bit isolated—to be on at least civil terms with the Blakes when they moved in. I've made approaches, not offensive ones, I hope, under the circumstances, but I sometimes have the feeling of a bell around my neck."

If he had been back on the newspaper, immersed in his job, Desmond would have written off Paula Blake's denial as one of the inexplicable things the world was full of—or even explicable; her husband had been standing there and she might not have told him about that trip—and reminded himself that people took unreasonable dislikes. But he was not technically at work, and one small mystery combined with another.

Mrs. Chilton could not be classed by any reasonable person as a bore or a nuisance. At sixty-plus she was full of projects but she did not harass people into group efforts; they were hers alone. Desmond knew from her disapproving daughter that, spurred on by a newspaper article, she had made a rug out of old stockings: "Isn't it hideous?" she said musingly of the result. Next, she had taken an evening class in shorthand offered by the high school—"One can take messages so more efficiently, d'you see." (She had apparently forgotten that she lived alone.) Someone had given her a biography of Schliemann, and she was currently enthralled with archeology, or, as she sensibly termed it, just plain digging.

This was the "old horror."

Desmond got out of bed, padded around in the dark, found cigarettes and matches on the desk beside his typewriter. Lydia Peel, honest, somehow vulnerable in spite of her unusual good looks, did not seem a soul mate of Paula Blake. As against that, she had been defensive tonight; she had clearly bitten back something about Paula's sister. He thought he could make a fairly good guess what.

And she didn't like Candide Chilton Blackwood. Desmond thoroughly enjoyed Candide: she was decorative, so transparently snobbish as to be almost appealing, and predatory. Although her divorce was pending and she had to behave with circumspection if she were to obtain custody of her valuable son, she had a built-in need to call herself to the attention of any male in her vicinity. Thus her summoning him to the telephone at the Donahue house tonight: "Desmond, would you be a lamb and pick up Mother's sleeping pills at the drugstore? I'd run in but Wendy Telfair has asked Harry and me for the night—her husband's away—and I'm bundling up all Harry's toys . . ."

Desmond, who had no idea who Wendy Telfair was, had wondered mildly about this gratuitous bit of detail from a woman who gave a strong impression of being a law unto herself. He also had a suspicion that no chronically bad sleeper, especially one living miles out of town in a Connecticut winter, would allow her supply of pills to go down to zero. He was borne out in this when, presently, he handed the new bottle to Mrs. Chilton and she thanked him in abstracted fashion. "I hope this wasn't a bother; it could easily have waited."

Candide had evidently not been very speedy with her bundling up of her son's toys. She was still struggling with the zipper of a canvas carry-all, and from the hard angry gestures of her hands Desmond hoped there was nothing very breakable inside. Harry, already coated in brass-buttoned dark blue, occupied this interlude by kicking with metronome regularity at the leg of a couch. When Mrs. Chilton remarked civilly, "I shouldn't do that, Harry," he lifted a flowerlike face under a mop of honey-colored hair and increased the speed and violence of his kicks.

It would have taken a dead man not to realize that he had interrupted something—as Candide had planned? Desmond said a hasty and general good night and took himself gratefully away.

He had smoked his cigarette at a living-room window that, in daylight, presented him with a brook at the foot of a sloping lawn; in his determination to keep his work divorced from his home, Edward Chilton had built the studio so that it faced away. Desmond went into the bathroom for aspirin and a glance at his watch—one-ten—and gazed automatically out the small high window.

As she often did, either waiting for her sleeping pill to take effect or hoping to drop off without resorting to one, Mrs. Chilton was reading late. The curtained glow had a tendency to pulse, tonight, and some nonsense about a failing light bulb went through Desmond's head before he realized that the bedroom window was not gold as usual but a muffled orange.

He snatched up the telephone, got a startled but efficient operator, thrust his bare feet into slippers, and, still coping with the sleeves of his raincoat, began to run across the dark field. The throbbing orange window watched him unworriedly, almost purring, like a cat which has plenty of time to kill the bird in its jaws.

The morning was gray, with a suggestion of snow in the making. Lydia slept late, because this was still a luxury and she had been awakened at some hour of the night by distant sirens. It was eleven o'clock before, scarfed and gloved against the wind, she reached Hopomoc Beach.

Such a goal on such a day, with smoke spinning out of chimneys, might have set a number of people to tapping their temples. But the major portion of eight summers of Lydia's life had been spent at this long stony crescent—it had always been diverting to watch weekending New Yorkers wincing along on the sides of their feet—and she had an almost physical thirst for the sight of open water. And here it was—but the welcome was not mutual. The Sound came swelling toward her, icily dark and as menacing as though it harbored sharks and wrecked ships, capped here and there, far out, with dangerous white. At full high tide, there were no friendly little expirations of foam but only a kind of devouring and lipless mumble against the stones.

Gulls circled patiently, white against the threatening sky, their cries a definition of cold and emptiness as they waited for the tide to recede and leave them its flung-up offerings. The floats had been beached against the winter storms and now, with their graying white tops roughened to sandpaper from spraying salt, and their seaweed-haired understructure of rust-red barrels, looked incapable of ever again tilting about in warm green waves. Lydia pushed her hands deeper into her pockets and shivered, marveling that she had ever swum so confidently in this water. She turned sharply at the sound of a car door slamming.

It was only a man and a woman who had come to look for driftwood and let their Irish setter run free, but Lydia's uneasy night had left its mark: for just a second, with the Volvo the only other car at the beach, she had had a feeling of real fright. She waved vaguely, received an answering wave, wondered if the Blakes knew about the beach as an occasional source of firewood ("This place is the devil to heat"), climbed back among the sliding stones and drove away.

In the town she bought a bottle of Scotch, so as not to leave the Donahues' liquor cabinet impaired, and then wandered along the shelves, wondering pensively what obscure drink Candide Chilton—no, Blackwood — would require when she came that afternoon with "a friend." Dubonnet came to mind, or Dry Sack. Lydia settled on the Dubonnet as something the Donahues would be more likely to finish up, collected a small crock of Cheddar cheese in port wine, and approached the counter.

She had not been listening consciously to the low conversation of two male customers there, but phrases had penetrated: "No, they say not, no sign at all . . ." "Well, it was always on the cards, with Margery. My God, though, what a ghastly way—"

The last speaker was a small elderly man in a rakishly belted trench coat and an outsize dark blue beret which appeared to have been borrowed from someone with a much bigger head. He had the haughty, frustrated look of a model whose vogue had passed. All voices fell silent as Lydia meekly proffered her Scotch and Dubonnet and cheese: like many New England towns with summer visitors, Elder's Farms liked its privacy during the winter.

But, driving home, she was able to place the little man as Arthur someone, the local institution no community is without. At sixteen Lydia had thought him to be at least eighty; from the slightly truer perspective of twenty-six she supposed he was approaching seventy.

He had posed as either a writer or an artist for so long that, perhaps because of the commanding size of his beret, he had finally been accepted as such without a word being printed or a picture hung. The Donahues had admired his fierce feuding spirit, and town meetings were said to come to crackling and enjoyable life when, no matter what the issue, Arthur stood up and demanded to be heard.

Lydia had a late lunch, inspected the living room critically, emptied and washed ash trays, did a little minor dusting. The wedding roses were browning and the carnations' spice was turning rank, so she threw them out. At the edge of the pond across the road she cut pussy willows; standing stiff and prim in their vases, they had an almost Japanese economy. It was three-thirty when the telephone rang.

Candide isn't coming after all, thought Lydia, and was not sure whether she felt relieved or let down. But what Candide said without preliminary was, "Lydia, I have the most enormous favor to ask you."

Lydia was not really surprised; any wonderment had lain in Candide's apparent eagerness to see her. They had certainly not, in the accepted sense of the phrase, been girls together. She said a little warily, "If I can, I will."

"Could I drop my little boy off with you for a while? I have to make a formal statement or a deposition or something, although I can't think why. I can hardly take Harry to the police station with me, and actually, there's no one else—"

Something of the total bewilderment at the other end of the line must have reached her then, because she said in a flat voice, "You haven't heard. My mother died in a fire last night, or rather very early this morning. After she swore to me, and I believed her," said Candide with what sounded like underlying anger, although telephones could be deceiving, "that she never smoked in bed."

Chapter 5

When Lydia had hung up, she wandered restlessly around the house, unable to sit down, feeling queerly stunned. All told, she had spent only about half an hour in Mrs. Chilton's company, but she had known people casually for months who had not left as vivid an impression.

The sirens in the night: had those been fire engines? And ". . . it was always on the cards, with Margery." Had that been spoken of Mrs. Chilton, who less than twenty-four hours ago had said with a snort of laughter that she would much rather go when she was facing something she loathed? She hadn't seemed like a woman who would endanger her daughter's and her grandson's lives as well as her own, but then smokers-in-bed doubtless felt confident of their ability to stay awake until the cigarette had been extinguished.

In the dining room, where a kind of homing instinct had made her pause, Lydia became aware of a strange sensation, almost like being on a stopped train when one next to it began to move gently. She went to a window and there was indeed motion outside: it was suddenly snowing, not the usual first practice flakes but a wind-slanted fall like fine white rain.

Early as it was, she had switched on the living-room lamps by the time Candide arrived with a small, fair, unwinking boy in brass-buttoned navy blue. Could this be the friend referred to so archly? During the ritual of gloved hand taking bare one briefly, and the automatic feminine phrases demanded after ten years even under the existing circumstances, Lydia reflected—in spite of stern resolutions to do no stock-taking—that time had done very little to Candide. Perhaps because she had had a world-weary air at nineteen, she looked uncannily the same. The almost ashen hair had darkened a little, and the snow and wind had brought a faint color to the bisque complexion, but as to mouth and eyes and general bearing, she might have been there to drawl, "Someone told me you were good with cars."

"—and this is your little boy," Lydia heard herself saying ridiculously, as though Candide might have changed her mind and brought her grandfather instead.

"Yes, this is Harry. *Harry!*" said Candide sharply, separating her son from the quiet study of a couch leg, and introductions were performed. Harry, instructed, began to take off his coat.

"Can I get you a glass of sherry or something, Candide, before you . . . ? You must be exhausted," said Lydia, observing with compunction the faint bruiselike blue under the haughty eyes.

"Yes, I am, rather, but no, thanks, not now. But you might—" Something changed in the slate-colored gaze. Candide glanced thoughtfully down at her son, who was now standing on one leg and swinging the other like a pendulum, and then up again. "Do you have a piano?"

"A—? Yes, in here." Sheer astonishment carried

Lydia over to the double white doors which, except on special occasions like the wedding party, cut the Donahues' vast living room in half. Surely Candide could not be going to sit down and play a little soothing music?

But, "There you go, darling," said Candide, and Lydia, who had stepped inside and switched on a lamp, stood back as Harry passed her as if she were a doorstop and marched across to the piano. To Lydia, because she had just remembered something Desmond Moran had said, he looked somewhat like a tiger approaching its dinner.

"Harry has such a leaning toward music," said Candide perfunctorily. A crash of wood indicated the piano lid being lifted. Still in her camel's-hair coat with a bronze and cream scarf at the throat, she sat on the very edge of a chair and leaned forward a little. "Actually, Harry and I weren't home at all last night," she said in a low, rapid voice. "Harry was spending the night with a friend of mine and he thinks I was too, and so do the police. There might be a bit of awkwardness, with the divorce pending, so I thought perhaps you wouldn't mind if I said I changed my plans and spent the night here with you."

With the part of her mind that was not transfixed with the casual audacity of this, Lydia thought that Candide needn't have been bothering to keep her voice so low with the banging discord issuing from the other room.

"It's the kind of thing that *might* have happened," Candide went on persuasively, "with your driving Mother home and my calling up afterward. If you had said that you were leaving town earlier than you'd expected, I might have explained to my friend that—"

"I'm sorry, Candide," said Lydia firmly, regretting

that she had let things get this far. Out of a number of reasons why not—that she had a strong dislike of being used and particularly being used like this, that Candide would not be telling this tale to a divorce lawyer but to the police, that as far as Lydia knew she was an utter stranger to the Donahues—she settled for, "This isn't my house, and I really couldn't lend it out like that."

Harry was now running up and down in front of the piano, striking flat-handedly all the way. It was an improvement. Candide's head went up and back imperiously; for a moment she was poised to say something cutting. Then, visibly like a woman having second thoughts about discarding a garment which she might want again someday, she stood up, pulled on her gloves, gave her brief unamused smile. "Oh, well, it was just a thought. I'll be back as soon as I can."

As soon as the front door had closed behind her, Lydia went into the other room and informed Harry that it was time to give the piano a rest. Most children asked "Why?" at such a juncture; Harry simply looked at her and went on pounding. "Watch your fingers," said Lydia briskly, and closed the keyboard and switched off the lamp.

In the middle of the living room, which he reached by dragging the tips of his shoes over the rug, Harry took a long, careful, 360-degree appraisal of the furnishings; for a ludicrous instant Lydia found herself being grateful that she had washed as well as emptied the ash trays. Then he said, watching keenly for the effect of this, "Grandmama"—he pronounced it with the accent on the last syllable—"got all burned up."

He couldn't be much over four. "Yes, I know."

"In a fire."

"It was *very* sad," said Lydia sternly, and Harry gave

her a noncommittal look out of his mother's eyes and, hands in the pockets of his suspender-strapped navy blue shorts, began to trudge purposefully around the border of the Oriental rug. "I sleeped at Wendy's house."

"That was nice. For Wendy, too," said Lydia brightly.

Harry turned a corner with precision. "Where did Mummy sleep?"

So in spite of Candide's confidence to the contrary, her son had his doubts. "She slept at Wendy's house too," said Lydia—she could do that much—and, to divert him and because the relentless tread around the rug's edge was beginning to get on her nerves, switched on the television set invitingly.

Strange, she thought (after explaining to Harry and feeling like a fool as she did so that the set was black-and-white because the Donahues didn't like color television), that the friend who seemed to have had no scruples about Candide's scheme beforehand should have backed out of it so sharply. Stranger still that the unknown Wendy had apparently declined to harbor Harry while Candide was with the police. He might not top anybody's list of people to be cast away with on a desert island, but there was after all sudden tragedy involved.

The telephone rang. Harry looked wildly around him, said, "I'll get it," and before Lydia could stop him had shot into the dining room. She closed her eyes and winced as she heard him say, "Miss Peel's residence," and then, incredibly, "Who's calling?"

He came back looking important. "It's Mrs. Blake."

If Paula Blake had been surprised, she didn't show it. "Lydia. I tried to call you earlier but the phone we use, the one at the gas station, has been out of order. I suppose we'll have to break down and get one. I imagine you've heard the ghastly news."

"About Mrs. Chilton. Yes, I was so sorry."

"So were we—poor old soul. I suppose I shouldn't say it, but the wonder is that it didn't happen sooner."

No, you shouldn't say it, not right now, thought Lydia—and Mrs. Chilton had *not* been a pitiful tottering wreck.

". . . too bad the daughter should have picked just that night to be away," Paula went on. "Desmond Moran—Mrs. Chilton's tenant—must have located her after he phoned in the alarm. The sirens woke us up, and when we realized where the fire was, Emmett drove over there to see if there was anything he could do. Apparently the daughter arrived when everything was all over, and then collapsed . . . Anyway, it's all very grim and of course I feel like a scoundrel because I wasn't very nice about her yesterday. Is it too late to suggest dinner tonight? To sort of get our minds off it?"

"Well, I have someone here right now," said Lydia, not wanting to alert Harry's attention by identifying him, "and I'm not sure exactly when—"

"That's right, your telephone service," said Paula,. sounding amused. "What about tomorrow night then? We could pick you up at seven."

Lydia said she would look forward to it and went back to the living room, toying with and discarding the idea of advising Candide's son that unless you were a butler or a business receptionist it was as well to answer the telephone with a simple hello. Although there was a suggestion of previous and speedy movement on the air, Harry was seated where she had left him, cross-legged on the floor, watching a laxative commercial in which a just-returned executive, arm fondly around his wife, was confiding to her his internal troubles in Pittsburgh. And they talk about the dangers of television violence, marveled Lydia, and asked Harry if he would like a glass of ginger ale. He nodded without looking away from the screen; apparently he didn't want to miss the part where the indulgent wife produced a large bottle from some private hoard.

Desmond Moran had known where to locate Candide; for some reason Lydia found that surprising. Come to that, why hadn't he—friend and confidant—volunteered to take charge of her son for an hour or two?

Lydia cut herself on the ice tray, poured ginger ale, realized belatedly that it was after five o'clock. She went rapidly back to the living room, but she was too late. The local news announcer was saying ". . . sixty-seven, widow of noted portrait photographer Edward Chilton and a long-time resident of Elder's Farms. The victim is believed to have been smoking in bed."

Lydia gazed cautiously at Harry's small delicately featured face. The television screen was the ultimate authority to the very young, and this would bring it home to him as nothing else seemed to have.

It did. Harry took his ginger ale carefully from her. He said pleasedly, with the air of not having quite believed it before, "Now I can have Grandmama's shubble."

The snow was beginning to lie on the roads when Desmond Moran drove away from the telephone company office with a number looked up in the Boston directory filed in his wallet. It was, he supposed, a form of counterirritant, because one very small but possibly vital thing had been swept away from him early that morning by water from a fireman's hose.

The Chilton house, as he drove by it on his way to the apartment, looked far too innocent to have swallowed a life. Except for black seepages around the door and onto the walls of the hall, the fire had been confined to Mrs. Chilton's bedroom, feeding luxuriously there on a down quilt, the bedding beneath, a whole wall of chintz curtains. The newspapers Desmond had felt obligated to tape over the picture window near the front door, having smashed it to gain entry a good three minutes before the fire engine and ambulance arrived, already wore a guileless furring of white.

He had seen enough fires to be sure that, with the bedroom door still closed when he arrived, Mrs. Chilton had succumbed to smoke inhalation. But there was always the tiny chance of escape into an adjoining bathroom, wet towels stuffed along the cracks, an elderly woman waiting in terror for help. Desmond pounded on the bedroom door, shouted Mrs. Chilton's name, snatched the door partway open even though he knew what the draft would do.

Flames tongued instantly out at him from the inner wall, a new billow blossomed behind them. Before he snapped the door shut again, he had time to see that Mrs. Chilton was dead, had probably been dead before he left the apartment. The shafted suction of air showed him something else: the bedside table with its clamshell ash tray, ironically left unscathed.

By the time a fireman's hose had been trundled in, and a second fireman had gone running through the house to make sure there were no other occupants even though Desmond said no, he had realized the significance of the ash tray—and it was too late. Impartially jetting water had stung the two or three cigarette butts out of the clamshell ash tray and then overturned it.

Even before the waiting ambulance men came in with their stretcher, Desmond had gone to the telephone; Candide could not be allowed to hear this, unwarned, on the morning news. The name Wendy Telfair was stamped in his memory as though she had intended it to be. There were only two Telfairs listed and he got the right one on the first try.

"Hello?" Voice reluctant with sleep; it was almost two o'clock.

"Mrs. Telfair? Is Mrs. Blackwood there? Tell her it's Desmond Moran, and that it's urgent."

"Hold on . . ."

Desmond held. Listening hard, he heard no retreating footsteps, no distant exhortations to anybody to wake up. Presently Mrs. Telfair said in an apologetic tone, "She's just getting her little boy quieted down after a nightmare. May I take a message for her?"

Desmond gave her the message, not brutally but not gently either; he wondered as he hung up how far away Candide was. Not far, as it turned out, allowing time to dress; she arrived half an hour later, and Desmond discovered for the first time that Emmett Blake was also on the scene. He looked as well-groomed as when Desmond had met him in the library, an accomplishment in view of slippered bare feet like Desmond's own. He said, "My God. I thought it might be a matter of carrying things out. I never dreamed—" and broke off with a quick shudder. He said with a glance at Candide, "I think she's going to faint."

In the course of his career Desmond had seen faints as well as fires, but none as graceful and gradual as Candide's. Never, in his experience, had a victim had the presence of mind to utter a doctor's name, but Candide murmured as she collapsed on the couch, "Dr. Nova."

Desmond telephoned Dr. Nova. Emmett Blake left, after offering sanctuary to Candide; she moved her head in a weary negative against a cushion. A police car arrived, alerted by the ambulance, and Desmond described to a sergeant the course of events. He said, drawing a cautious length of the room away from Candide, "I know what this looks like, Officer, but I think it's questionable that Mrs. Chilton was at fault. She was a careless smoker, granted, but she was well aware of it. I saw her bedside ash tray before the firemen got here—it's a clamshell, and it was snow-white."

The sergeant gave him a blank look and then a quick mystified shake of his head.

"With a glass ash tray, you can stub out a cigarette and scrape around with it and leave the glass perfectly clear except for the ashes under the butt. You can't do that with a clamshell," said Desmond. "Putting out a cigarette leaves black tracks, and there were none. In spite of two or three cigarette ends, I saw them."

"So?" said the sergeant, gazing compassionately down the room at the pale Candide.

"So it's possible that someone might have put cigarette butts in an empty ash tray to make it look as though Mrs. Chilton had fallen asleep with a burning cigarette."

"With the front door locked, you said that yourself," said the sergeant, "and we've had a look at the back door and the windows and there's no sign of tampering. Anyway, who's doing all this? Why?"

Desmond was saved from a non-answer by the arrival of Dr. Nova, a portly man not far from retirement. He gave Candide, who was now weeping quietly, two tiny tablets, said summarily that she must not be questioned, and departed. The sergeant offered gallantly to drive Candide back to her friend's house; she would want to be with her little boy. Desmond found himself alone in an acrid-smelling house with a wind rising. In Mrs. Chilton's pantry he found old newspapers, hunted down Scotch tape in a kitchen drawer, blocked off the window temporarily.

He had been in search of aspirin when he first saw that pulsing window, but it was no use—after seeing the blackened form half-in and half-out of the bed, as though Mrs. Chilton had struggled to free herself of the bedclothes before the smoke caught up with her—sending an infant to do a man's work. He made himself an unmeasured drink, and fell asleep as it was getting light.

Now, the Boston number that he called, listed for Emmett Blake in the still-current Boston directory, rang without answering. The new tenant or tenants must work and not be home yet, as it was hard to believe that an apartment at this particular address hadn't been snapped up immediately.

Next, Desmond called his newspaper. Fidge Duffy had been the photographer assigned to him for the Mardi Gras coverage three years ago, but nobody had ever been christened Fidge. A friendly switchboard girl told him after a short wait that it was Aloysius Duffy, and gave him the number.

By a small miracle, Fidge was at home. After an exchange of pleasantries conducted over the bouncy sounds of young children and some deep-throated barking, Desmond asked, "Who was it that we fell in with at the Mardi Gras that time, fell being the operative word?" and Fidge said snappily, "Where were you on the night of June sixteenth?" and took time for thought. He said eventually, "Big guy, blond. Some kind of salesman, or representative as they like to be called. Michaelson? Nicholson?"

Nicholson shot home like something into a slot. "Thanks. There was a woman with him," said Desmond tensely. "Reddish-brown hair, green eyes, maybe thirty. There was some kind of fall-out the next day."

The dog continued to bark, the children to squeal. "The next day," said Fidge with feeling, "I was trying to keep my head from flying off my shoulders, bang, every time I put my feet down. Of all the blanks I've ever drawn, that's the blankest. Why the interest in the woman, in your dilapidated state?"

"I've come across her again, but she says not. If you remember anything about her, call me, will you? Collect."

Desmond gave his number and hung up. He tried the Boston number again.

Lydia went to bed early. She had been detachedly interested in Candide's serene return—she had clearly thought of something to tell the police—and was not surprised when, instead of hoping that Harry had not been a bother, Candide said to her son, "Yes, darling, I know you want to go home, but Mummy is going to have a drink first. I talked to that nice sergeant who drove me back to the Telfairs'," she added to Lydia.

How very simple, thought Lydia, especially in view of Candide's slightly superior accent; the sergeant had naturally assumed that she had come from there, and no question would arise at all. Candide took a delicate sip of her martini and said with the faintest of frowns, "I know that Desmond Moran is a newspaperman, but I don't think it's kind of him to try and stir things up about the fire. I think it's quite *cheap.*"

"How is he trying to do that?" inquired Lydia.

"Oh, something about an ash tray," said Candide pettishly. "As if there wouldn't be an ash tray. Fortunately nobody's paying any attention, because otherwise the insurance—"

Incredibly, she meant it—and heard herself, and gave Lydia a smile which she had wanned, if there could be such a verb. "Really, at this point I don't know what I'm saying. It's all been so frightful."

Lydia rose automatically as Candide buttoned Harry into his coat. She said, drawing on every ounce of Christian charity, "If you don't want to go back to the house tonight, Candide, there's lots of room here," but Candide shook her head. Luckily, it did not seem to cross her mind to accept on Harry's behalf. "People will be calling. Come along, darling . . ."

Something about an ash tray; was Desmond Moran possibly thinking that the fire hadn't been accidental? But that would argue somebody knowing that Mrs. Chilton would be alone in the house, being admitted by her—the news report had been straightforward, with no hint of forced entry—and then . . . Lydia discovered that she did not want to think any further in that direction.

Just before she slept, she went back to Harry's peculiar reaction to the televised mention of his grandmother's death, and her own repeated *"Shubble?"*

Harry had given her an angry look, as though he wasn't often caught in mispronunciation. "What you dig with."

So—and why was it disturbing, bordering on the unpleasant?—Grandmama's shovel.

Chapter 6

At some point during the night a winter-weakened hickory bough came crashing down on the roof. For a long dream-tangled moment it sounded like someone trying to burrow into the house from above, and Lydia lay rigid and immobilized in bed, mind racing along with her heart. The total silence that had followed was either reassuring or immensely dangerous. Then the dream fell away completely, and she threw back the covers and crossed to the raised window and looked out and up at the projecting end of a leafless branch.

In its own frosty exhalation of light, the pond wore an unflawed cover of snow. But suppose, thought Lydia, who was sometimes given to these fascinated if horrified small-hours reflections, there had been new tracks across it, emerging toes-first from the pussy willows directly across the road?

This was Desmond Moran's work, she told herself grimly, going back to bed. Because he had raised a question about the origin of a fatal fire she was, for the first time since her arrival in Elder's Farms, sharply aware that she was alone in a fairly big house, and that by this time a lot of people must know it. (Mrs. Chilton, now being readied at a mortuary, had been alone.)

There were three doors, four if you counted the outside cellar door—but I won't count that one, said Lydia firmly to herself. She had never liked the Donahues' cellar, a place, it seemed to her, where faceless people were flattened against walls just around the corner, and what appeared to be shadows were momentarily stilled shapes. Once, when she was twelve or thirteen and investigating a new litter of tiger kittens, the mother cat's eyes had swelled in a sudden stare and Lydia had become so panicked that she fell *up* the stairs, scraping a knee.

The inside cellar door opened into the dining room, under the enclosed stairway. And it was bolted. And she was, she knew very well, going to have to get up and go downstairs and make sure; she had simply been putting it off.

The bolt was in place, as common sense had told her it would be; the house, waked briefly to lamplight, was tranquil and safe in the snow. But Mrs. Chilton, once resurrected, was not willing to lie down again so soon. Lydia, back under her warm covers, heard her say to Emmett Blake as she donned the raincoat with the cigarette holes in it, "Do think, won't you, about what we've been discussing? Your cousin Simon did agree, I assure you."

The acquisition of more antiques?

But a little later, in the Volvo, Mrs. Chilton had told Lydia that Simon Wister had been a very family-minded man—"It would never have occurred to him to leave so much as a stick or a stone elsewhere"—and she had sounded approving.

Still, the world was full of misunderstandings. Maybe Mrs. Chilton had thought that the Blakes, occupied only at easel and typewriter, needed the money. Lydia had a brief half-dream of an antique shovel in an old carved chest and was thoroughly asleep.

The Western Union office was small and chatty, and by the next day it was known that Candide Blackwood had received condolences from her soon-to-be-ex-husband in New York and her parents-in-law, the Harrison Blackwoods, in Philadelphia.

"There's money there, to put it mildly," Desmond Moran told Lydia knowledgeably over a noon drink at the Hopomoc Inn, "and if she minds her manners Candide is apt to see a good bit of it. Harry—not as in Tom, Dick or, obviously—is the only grandchild and pretty sure to stay that way. Blackwood's in his sixties."

And manners-minding in this context, thought Lydia, gazing down at her whiskey sour, seemed to imply sleeping where you said you were sleeping—which of course Desmond Moran knew all about, having been able to put his finger on Candide the night of the fire.

The day was very cold and beautiful, purple-skied, with tawny field grass poking through the six-inch fall of snow and beards of white hung prodigally among lilacs and firs and barberry bushes. Lydia, who was rapidly tiring of cold roast beef and turkey and also needed cigarettes, had told herself that the Volvo was designed for just these conditions; still, not daring to mingle closely with natives who drove as though the roads were bare, she had left the car parked on a quiet side street just outside the town and walked the rest of the way. She had found a pair of boots which were a size too big, as she was not as tall as any of the Donahues, and astonishingly uncomfortable. When Desmond's rented car pulled up beside her, she got in gladly.

He owed her a drink and at least lunch, he said, but

where did she want to go first? He accompanied her to the supermarket, where she bought cigarettes, lamb chops, milk, romaine, a tomato which looked like a cunning wax replica. Desmond studied her basket and got himself some lettuce and, after suspicion and consultation with her, some thin spaghetti; his last package, he said, had exploded into one-inch lengths.

The communal basket had a domestic air, and Lydia saw or imagined glances cast at them; this was, after all, a small town not out of the grip of winter. At the moving-belt counter, Desmond hoisted his lettuce and spaghetti free from Lydia's purchases and said cheerfully, "Now, your friends the Blakes usually do it the easy way. A once-a-week order from Chase's, delivered."

A woman ahead of them had tendered a check which called for managerial approval. Lydia, getting out cash, said lightly, "Well, so would I in their place. They're both trying to work at home, which I suspect isn't as simple as it sounds."

A manager with a mustache like a thicket arrived, gave the woman with the check an X-ray glance, scrawled, and went away. The woman wanted twenties, tens and fives, handed back a five and received ones, stowed the bills carefully in her wallet, started to leave, and decided to get change.

"She's going to want six 1910 dimes and the rest in Indian-head pennies," murmured Desmond, gazing politely at pyramided cans. "What's Blake's work like?"

He was still assuming that she knew the Blakes well. Lydia disabused him with a faint crispness. "I have no idea, having met them for the first time the day before yesterday. It's Paula's sister I know, in Santa Fe. I'm seeing them tonight, so I suppose I could ask. Putting it tactfully."

. . . And now he was talking about Candide. Lydia finished her drink, which was tart and good, and said directly, "Candide said you brought up something about an ash tray with the police. Do you really think there was something peculiar about the fire?"

Desmond had had his eye on a waiter. He raised his eyebrows at Lydia, signaled for a return of whiskey sours, and said with a thoughtful air, "I did at first, but that was reaction. When something like that happens to someone you like, there's a tendency to insist that it couldn't have been her own fault."

His gaze was clear and unflickering. "The local paper doesn't come out until tomorrow, but the editor told me Mrs. Chilton had taken two sleeping pills, not that that'll be mentioned. I picked up a new bottle for her that night, and the label directions call for one. So . . ."

He shrugged. Lydia was conscious of a deep relief. Although she had instructed her mind not to dwell on the alternative, she had known that for it to appear that she had died of her own carelessness when in fact the fire had been deliberately set, Mrs. Chilton would have had to be rendered unconscious so that smoke inhalation could kill her. Since any traceable violence would be out of the question, something like a pillow held over her face—Lydia moved her shoulders a little, as if a cold cloak had touched her, and settled down to enjoy her lunch.

When he was not in his bloodhound mood, Desmond Moran was very good company. Lydia learned that he was in Elder's Farms winding up sick leave after injuries in a plane crash—he was brief about that; that he had a younger brother, the cause of his godfather duties the other day, and an older sister and a problem manuscript. Lydia told him about her mission with the mirror which had required a courier and, occupied with her clams, did not notice the sudden intensity of his gaze. To her surprise, but still instinctively cautious enough to keep Susan McGrath's identity out of it, she heard herself describing the problem in the Santa Fe gallery.

"Security guards are expensive for a small place, and they tend to put some people off in a shop where it's really necessary to stand around and contemplate and even handle things. Besides, the actual thefts are secondary."

"You mean a man who would steal from a woman under the circumstances might very well have future delights up his sleeve, like an existing wife or wives," said Desmond, pursuing ramifications and introducing to Lydia an aspect she hadn't even thought of, "but the bad news ought to be broken by a disinterested third party, so that your friend can act on it or not as she pleases." He lit cigarettes for them both. "Does the gallery have any copyable paintings?"

". . . Yes," said Lydia, wondering after an instant why this solution hadn't occurred to her. Establish an observant young art student there . . .

It came as a distinct little jar to realize that Desmond had dropped two casual glances to his watch. Lydia wished for one of her own to consult so that she could utter a cry of horror at some missed appointment; failing that, she was instantly into her coat. At the Volvo, when her groceries had been transshipped, Desmond waited until the engine had caught obediently. "You're going to be here for a few more days, aren't you?" he asked, and, when she said yes, "I have to be out of town one day, maybe two, but I'll see you when I get back."

It was brisk, absent, taken-for-granted, as though

they had known each other for months. But in spite of his offhandedness, what Lydia thought of as his detective mood seemed to be stealing over him again, although he hadn't mentioned the Blakes at all during lunch and certainly his look of relief, when he told her about Mrs. Chilton's extra sleeping pill on the night of the fire, had mirrored her own. It did not cross her mind that his relief might have had quite a different cause.

The camera that always rode with her on the passenger seat was a reminder that she ought to be taking pictures—who knew when she would be East again?—but it was an unsophisticated one and the light hadn't been propitious. She might manage to capture the Blakes' house in this built-in brilliance of snow, as Susan had asked her to, but they had no telephone and, after her earlier reception, Lydia would not have cared to be surprised in their driveway, Instamatic to eye. Well, it was an intrusion, in a way; certainly the pueblo Indians felt strongly about it.

She drove home, put away the groceries, was surprised to find that it was after two-thirty. Her feet were delighted to be out of the boots. Although a cleaning woman's ministrations lasted far longer than any private efforts, it was time to do something about the house, and she cleaned the kitchen and then got out the vacuum, reflecting on the mysterious but eternal truth that there was no drudgery in housework on other people's premises. As a fringe benefit, there was none of the pervasive, wind-driven New Mexico sand and dust to cope with here; a perfunctory flourish with a mop sufficed.

Should she or should she not call Candide and ask in

the usual hollow phrase if there were anything she could do? Might not that land her with piano-playing Harry? On the other hand, equal to the occasion and even cool about it as she seemed, Candide had lost a parent under horrifying circumstances. Duty prevailed, and Lydia telephoned.

How sweet of her, Candide said, and it was unfortunate that her slight disdainful smile seemed to travel accurately along the wire. "Actually, if I can do a bit of arranging, might I meet a friend there later on, just to get out of this house? He might arrive earlier than I do —say five?" Her voice vanished briefly, said in an impatient aside, "Harry would *love* a bath, Laura, he just wants coaxing," and came back, sounding amused and patronizing. "We're to be married as soon as it's possible, if that quiets your scruples."

Lydia's hard-won compassion went up in smoke. She said, gazing steadily at the opposite wall, "Candide, I'd hate to think you were remarrying just because of *me,*" and had the satisfaction of listening to a few seconds of outraged silence. Then Candide said with a false little laugh, "Well . . . not quite, shall we say. It's confidential, by the way. I'll see you later, then . . ."

Why here, wondered Lydia dismally; the Telfairs had clearly opted out of the situation, but why not a motel outside of town or some other place suitably divorced from the public eye? Because you're available, of course, and all is grist to Candide's mill.

At four-thirty, making a meticulous note to call the charge operator immediately afterward, she telephoned Susan in Santa Fe.

"Lydia!" With all those miles and mountains in between, Susan might have been around the corner.

"How are you, and how is everything there?"

"Fine, but snowy. I wanted to let you know that the mirror arrived intact, and your sister loves it." Not true, thought Lydia curiously, examining this for the first time. There had been admiring exclamations, and trial placements against various walls, but not one moment of deep, genuine pleasure.

"I'm so glad. Paula's fine, I gather. How do you like Emmett?"

Having been informed of her sister's marriage only two days before the event, Susan had never met her brother-in-law of four years although she had often talked to him in the course of holiday and birthday calls.

"He's very nice, and quite attractive," said Lydia, hearing an eerie echo of the all-purpose description she had given the Blakes of Miles Marsh. Well, what *did* you say? "I'm having dinner with them tonight, in fact. Any messages?"

"Just love, and make sure you bring home some pictures."

"I will. No more trouble at the gallery, I hope?"

"Well, that little oval of Napoleon you liked so much has disappeared. I've rearranged things completely, though—some really beautiful stuff came down from Taos—so it may just have been misplaced. Eloy isn't the most methodical of helpers, as you know."

"Oh. Because I thought—" Lydia broached Desmond's art-student ploy, and held her breath because of something he had said in the car driving away from the inn: "If your friend says, 'What a horrible suggestion,' or words to that effect, maybe she knows more than you think she does."

But Susan said thoughtfully, "That's a good idea. Apart from the first stare to see how they're doing, people forget copyists are there." She paused. "I'm not entirely sure, Lydia, but you might all drink a small toast to us tonight. Just in case."

"We will," said Lydia. It was all she could bring herself to say.

Desmond Moran arrived in Boston's South Station at six o'clock that evening. After twenty minutes of infighting he got a cab, checked in at his hotel, resisted the temptation of a drink after the rattling journey, and was on his way to 26 Belnight Street.

He had finally succeeded in reaching the tenant of the erstwhile Blake apartment the evening before, and been rewarded with the information that the superintendent was on the premises from 4 P.M. until midnight. "But if it's a question of getting your heat turned up," said the female voice which had evidently been sipping something other than tea, "you'd be better off with me, honey."

Belnight Street was on the lower reaches of Beacon Hill, and No. 26 was, like its neighbors, white-painted brick with black accents over its windows, a canopy, skeletal magnolia trees in front. The Blakes had certainly been doing well for themselves in Boston. Prudently armed with a bottle of Scotch—in his experience building superintendents were irascible about being disturbed above and beyond the course of duty—Desmond pressed the appropriate bell.

Chapter 7

When Lydia opened the door to Candide's friend at shortly after five o'clock (evidently the friend referred to on the first occasion, but for some reason that arrangement had fallen through), it was instantly clear why, under the circumstances, she preferred to meet him privately. She might as well have hoped to go out inconspicuously with a midget or a practicing cannibal.

Jones Haviland—even Lydia, who did not follow art news closely, knew that he was the most fashionable portrait painter on the East coast—gave an impression of more bulk than he actually possessed, but that was minor. The glossily bald brown crown of his head rose out of his amber hair—locks to his shoulders, sweeping beard with two dramatic pale streaks which might or might not have been the work of peroxide—like an egg from an eggcup. His round bright eyes had a stabbing effect. He wore a pea jacket, denims, sneakers, and an Italian silk shirt. Lydia guessed him to be approaching fifty.

His first action after acknowledging her was to clasp his hands behind his back and make a slow reflective survey of the room; Lydia found herself thinking that he would get along very well with Harry. "Charming," he said finally in a voice as surprising as if a mastiff had let out a chirp. "I like it."

"Thank you," said Lydia equably. She had made a few fast mental adjustments. Candide gave a strong impression of being oriented more toward Savile Row tailoring and bench-made shoes—but this was Jones Haviland, so denims and sneakers had sudden cachet. "Shall we wait for Candide, Mr. Haviland, or may I get you a drink right away?"

There was a small but trying percentage of people who did not answer direct questions, and Jones Haviland belonged to it. "Candide is off making the usual barbarous arrangements," he said, flinging himself dangerously onto the couch and fixing Lydia with an accusatory stare. "She's having to be very brave."

Lydia murmured suitably and then, as a silence threatened to extend itself, was foolish enough to ask if he had known Mrs. Chilton well.

"Of course, Mrs. Chilton was firmly in the Blackwood camp, so I was anathema. Too bad, I rather liked her," said Haviland pensively. He appeared to brood. "The circumstances are painfully reminiscent. I lost my second wife in a fire—a combination of hair spray and a lighted match, apparently."

"How dreadful," said Lydia sympathetically, and Haviland re-crossed his sneakered feet and said with an air of wanting to be fair, "Yes. But it was years ago. It is why"—he glanced distastefully at the ash tray near his elbow—"I no longer smoke."

"I can certainly understand that, but," said Lydia, seized by a feeling that she was being manipulated by two people whom she cared nothing about, "I hope you don't mind if I do."

Candide arrived, pale but composed in a chestnut

cape which revealed a suit of honey-colored wool beneath. She said, "Lydia, you are a lamb. Jones, darling, you look the tiniest bit tired. I think you're overworking, and you did promise me you wouldn't."

Lydia escaped to the kitchen, where she wondered to herself, What hath God wrought? The arrogant Candide was soft and almost humble; she gave an impression of sitting at the painter's feet and gazing adoringly up into his face. Possibly he had once taken a thorn out of her foot. They murmured together in the living room, and as this seemed to be the point of the whole business, Lydia took her time over fixing drinks: a martini for Candide, Dubonnet for Jones Haviland, a long and watery Scotch for herself, as she would be dining with the Blakes. Preparing cheese and crackers gave her another interval away, but by this time she had learned that the painter was driving to Marblehead tonight; he had a commission there and would be gone for two weeks.

. . . Small wonder, now, about all this secrecy. Mrs. Chilton had sided with her son-in-law in the matter of the divorce, Candide's custody of her child was contingent upon her interim behavior; Jones Haviland's wife had died by fire. Combined with the absence of Candide and Harry on the night when Mrs. Chilton had met a similar death, these facts would make a feast for Elder's Farms. People were apt to turn the most swiftly on the exotic members in their midst, even though matricide occurred mainly in Greek plays.

Lydia, appalled at the turn of her own thoughts, was especially cordial to Candide and Haviland as they prepared to leave in their separate cars. Candide told her that the funeral would be at eleven o'clock at the Episcopal church the next day. Haviland, who had subjected her to an intense scrutiny for the past ten minutes, informed her that if he were painting her he would put green highlights in her hair and that she must never, accordingly, wear green because of tonal conflicts. Lydia, who owned a muted green tweed coat of which she was very fond, assured him tranquilly that she would not.

. . . How very softly you could proceed into a house in sneakers, if you had Candide's key. Or how easy to return, knowing about the sleeping pills, and call lullingly, "It's me, Mother; I forgot Harry's bathrobe," or toothbrush, or some other item . . . But of course nobody had come. A burning cigarette had slipped from Mrs. Chilton's fingers and smoldered unnoticed until it was too late. Even Desmond, the first on the scene and the original entertainer of doubts, agreed that it was accidental.

But at no time, Lydia realized, had she said to herself that Candide was incapable of such an act.

"These are my festive, going-out glasses," remarked Paula Blake at seven-thirty. "I suppose contact lenses would be even more festive, but the very thought makes my eyes water."

Lydia knew that Susan McGrath, with recently acquired contact lenses, had exhorted her sister with the zeal of a convert but in vain. "They're very attractive," she said with truth. Paula had the kind of face which glasses actually became, and the owlish blue lenses seemed to wake up red lights in her hair.

"This is the most mysterious place," said Emmett, glancing around the restaurant. "Everybody in the kitchen must come to work in six cars."

It was a phenomenon which Lydia had come across

before, and for which there was no doubt some explanation. Although the parking lot of the restaurant five miles out of town had been so crowded as to suggest a wait, the big pleasant low-ceilinged dining room in which they occupied a booth was less than half full. But the drinks were honest and the food good, the Blakes had assured her, and they had thought she might like to see someplace other than the Hopomoc Inn.

After her earlier company they seemed brisk, nice, uncomplicated. Paula said that they had finally hung the mirror between the two west windows in the living room and that it looked stunning there, reflecting a small luster vase on the mantel. Lydia, who had had the event driven from her mind by the advent of Jones Haviland and then Candide, told them that she had spoken to Susan that afternoon.

"You mean before the rates went down?" asked Emmett, sounding scandalized, and Paula put down her drink and groped for cigarettes in her handbag instead. "You told her we love the mirror, I hope. What news on the romantic front?"

"She mentioned that a toast might be in order."

"Toasts are always so embarrassing, but how *wonderful,*" said Paula. "Isn't it, Emmett?"

"Never having met Susan face to face, and never having met this Miles at all, I'll stick with saying that I certainly hope it is," said Emmett a trifle dryly. "Lydia appears to have reservations."

She had been half-prepared for this. "It's just that Susan's known him for such a short time," she said, "and he's so eligible to be lying on the ground like a gold nugget or something." Aware of something close to a bridle behind Paula's blue glasses, she added hastily, "Some fairly strange people drift in and out of Santa Fe, so I suppose I'm falling over backwards being cautious."

Dinner arrived then, to her physical relief as well; her steamed clams seemed very far back in time and she had missed the salad served first in the Southwest, or even the basket of tostados with a little dish of searingly hot sauce for dipping. The Blakes decided that the occasion called for a bottle of wine, and at the same time put forward the suggestion that Susan wasn't, after all, a naive nineteen.

Lydia was faintly puzzled by their reaction. As Susan's sister and brother-in-law they would naturally wish her well, but their obvious pleasure seemed to hold a tinge of relief, like that of Victorian parents whose browning-around-the-edges daughter finally had prospects.

Something of this must have showed, because Paula said, "Don't you dare tell Susan, but I've worried about her on and off ever since Bill died—she came awfully close to the kind of crack-up that never gets put together again. She isn't really a loner, she's enormously domestic-minded—well, you'd know, and that can't be much fun for a woman alone. I'd like nothing better than to see her happily married again . . . *damn.*"

In reaching down for her escaped napkin, she had moved too precipitately, and the handbag on the banquette beside her tumbled to the floor. Emmett rose from the other end of the curved seat and retrieved coins and a rolling lipstick; Lydia bent for something that had skittered to her feet. It was a letter stamped for mailing, and the typed address—Bureau of Vital Records, Philadelphia, Pa.,—did not register until Paula, taking it from her, said with an air of vexation, "We forgot this thing again, Emmett—I'll never have a birth certificate at this rate. Mine got lost in the moving," she explained to Lydia, "or at least I haven't been able to find it, and it doesn't seem a very wise thing to be without. Not that I need it for any exciting purpose like a passport—we certainly won't be going anywhere until we've gotten somewhere with our work, which I find difficult without the dear old overseer and lash. Emmett's much better about that than I am."

With Desmond in mind, it seemed an opportune time for Lydia to ask what kind of painting he did.

"Fabulous," said Paula succinctly, but Emmett clarified this into oils, landscape and still life. A short silence fell, with the stifling effect of a cushion. Nobody mentioned Susan's gallery. Lydia broke it by asking if they knew Jones Haviland.

"Just to meet. God, how that man is cleaning up—and he deserves it," said Emmett in devout tones. "He looks like a phony, in fact even his beard looks phony, but he's marvelous."

So Candide had been successful in her strategy: even this alert pair knew of no involvement. On the other hand, according to Desmond, they almost never went into the town. Lydia thought that the evening would pass with no mention whatever of Mrs. Chilton, which would be odd as they had all been with her several hours before her death, until Paula said abruptly as they were driving back to the Donahue house, "We sent flowers for Mrs. Chilton, by the way, but I doubt that we'll go to the funeral. We didn't know her all that well, and we *hate* funerals—in fact, we've decided to live forever so as to spare our friends. That's a complication you don't have to worry about, anyway."

On the contrary, Lydia said; Mrs. Chilton's daughter that very afternoon had stressed the time and place of the funeral, so she felt more or less obligated. To the concentrated silence in the car—the roads were slippery and Emmett was having to drive with considerable care—she added that she had driven Mrs. Chilton home from the Blakes' on the day they first met, and thereby come into contact with Candide again.

"Emmett says she's very attractive," said Paula in a neutral and wifely way, and, "Darling, *watch* it!"

The bridge was negotiated successfully, but Lydia realized that the other residents of Elder's Farms, no matter how nonchalantly they drove at noon, had respect for a snowfall which had melted a little at about three o'clock and then re-frozen; they hadn't passed a single other car.

She had had the wit to leave lights on, not only in the living room, so that the house looked tenanted and welcoming. The Blakes took her up promptly on her offer of a liqueur—they had often admired the place from the outside—but did not stay long, mercifully. In some way that Lydia could not define, they were enervating people to be with over a period of hours. They were critical and zestful in their criticism; no subject was small enough to escape judgment.

At the door Paula said, "If we shouldn't see you again before you leave—"

"Oh, I almost forgot. Susan wants a picture of your house, and of both of you, and I promised," said Lydia, trying not to ripple with shivers in the icy air. "If tomorrow is decent at all, could I come by at a non-working hour?"

"Certainly. I sent Susan an awful picture of Emmett, with a lot of his head missing, which couldn't be said to do him justice. We're not great ones for picture taking," said Paula, "so any time after one would be fine. How about three? That seems to be the optimum hour if there is one in March."

Lydia waved good-bye, closed and locked the door, was gratefully in bed ten minutes later. She wondered, just before she went to sleep, what Desmond Moran was doing.

"Well, did you?" asked Paula Blake as they drove away. "I wasn't watching, naturally."

"I certainly did."

"I think it went off very well, all things considered, even though she had to see that damned letter. Let's drop it in a mailbox tonight, by the way, if we can find one."

"People lose important documents all the time when they move," Emmett pointed out.

"I thought you were going to have us off that bridge. I take it you were thinking what I was."

"Yes, and we were both wrong." Emmett whistled his six notes again and they laughed together in the moving darkness, curiously twinlike, daintily malicious.

"Anyway, she'll soon be on her merry way home with her snapshots," said Paula presently. "We must remember to pose prettily . . ."

Chapter 8

The superintendent of the Boston apartment building was unpromising from the outset. Small, lantern-jawed, diluted brown eyes full of fiery grievance under whiskery gray brows, J. Harney had the general aspect of a fox terrier in a bad mood. He listened wintrily to Desmond's tale of having come to Boston to look up the Blakes on behalf of mutual friends, said with fierce satisfaction that they had moved out right after Christmas and that was all *he* knew; he minded his own business and it was a pity everybody didn't. Pinned by Desmond's eye, he stumped off with the Scotch and returned with drinks that looked like the remains of drinks.

"But they must have left an address with you," said Desmond, sitting down uninvited on a cement couch slip-covered in brown. "Friends they'd forgotten to notify would have come looking for them."

The superintendent showed teeth of such falsity that he might have run them up himself in an idle hour. "Well, they didn't."

But it seemed impossible that there was no information at all to be gleaned from what was usually a rich source, and Desmond was not ready to leave yet. "Then they've certainly left my friends' clock in storage here," he said authoritatively. "One of those glass clocks, electric, with no works showing."

Clear memories of a confiscated bone appeared to recur to Harney; his tan eyes flashed excitably. "They didn't leave no such a clock. Neat as a pin, they had that place, *and* moving a week earlier than they said they was going to. You can tell your friends that for me."

"Then they took the clock with them by mistake," said Desmond pacifically. "Natural enough, having to change their plans like that. I suppose the new tenant was demanding occupancy?"

The lantern jaw came forward, suggesting that nothing was demanded successfully in any building superintended by J. Harney. "They just decided to leave early. Any law against that?"

"Not that I know of." Desmond stood. A generous honorarium from the Blakes had crossed his mind, but in fairness he had encountered people like Harney before, in milder forms: they lived in a world in which common courtesy was inspired by sinister motives and the giving out of any information whatever would lead them into the jaws of the Internal Revenue Service or worse. He had his hand on the doorknob when the superintendent said suspiciously, "Who are these friends of yours, anyway?"

"The Nicholsons," said Desmond, because it was a name never far out of his mind in this connection, and the whiskery eyebrows took a leap and then a plunge.

"They couldn't have thought much of their clock then," said Harney with sour triumph, "seeing as how they was here a couple of nights before the Blakes moved out."

* * *

It was like being tapped smartly under the ribs by a hand he hadn't seen coming. "Really?" inquired Desmond, letting go of the doorknob and not having to try for astonishment. "How strange that they didn't tell me." He allowed doubt to creep in. "Of course, Nicholson isn't such an unusual name. My friends are in their thirties, he's quite heavy and walks with a limp—"

But he was not going to get any descriptions all the more detailed because of Harney's truculence. The superintendent nipped agilely around Desmond, snatched at the doorknob, said, "Wrong people, mister, and I got work to do," and slammed the door in a manner indicating that it would reopen in a matter of seconds and the almost-untouched bottle of Scotch come flying out. It did not.

In the small high-ceilinged lobby, which contained only two straight chairs flanking a marble-topped table with a lamp, plus what looked at first glance like a tastefully framed sampler but was in fact a stern prohibition of children and pets, Desmond glanced consideringly at his watch. The building contained eight apartments, two to a floor, but he suspected that his best bet among the tenants lay with the Blakes' neighbors in 4B, the Morrows, with whom they would have waited for and shared the self-service elevator if nothing more. At not much after seven-thirty they might be in the middle of dinner; on the other hand, if he waited until after his own dinner—

Deservedly, after his session with the superintendent, his luck was in. The Morrows proved to be a sober, graying, fiftyish couple—small hope of much social intercourse here—and Desmond warmed to them at once because of a jaunty and obviously contraband blue parakeet in a wicker cage. The tale of the clock had somehow lost its luster downstairs, so he told them that he was trying to locate a friend of his sick brother's who had also, he believed, been a friend of the Blakes. They were as amiable and unsuspicious as Harney had been hostile, although, they said, they doubted if they could help him.

"We scarcely knew the Blakes; they were younger than we are and you know how it is in apartment buildings," said Morrow, lighting a pipe to go with the after-dinner coffee which had been offered to and declined by Desmond, who was looking forward to a respectable drink and wanted nothing cluttering up its way. "Good morning or good night in the elevator or the lobby, that was about it. They did introduce us to some people called Nicholson, but I don't remember the first name."

Mrs. Morrow had closed her eyes tightly in an obvious effort at recollection. Desmond called down curses on the head of the blue parakeet, which chose that moment to burst into distracting trills and flutters, but she was evidently used to these interruptions because she said promptly, opening her eyes, "Philip, I think. Yes, Philip, I'm sure."

"Tall fellow, fair-haired?" invited Desmond, and there was a mild discussion between the Morrows, who had been introduced to him on the street outside on a rainy night while they were waiting for taxis, but yes, they finally agreed, he had been blond. His wife had been wearing a close-fitting rain hat, but their impression was that she had been blonde too.

"Did they see a good deal of the Blakes, do you know?"

"Well, sometimes. On and off." Morrow let it hang there, curiously inconclusive.

The parakeet had stopped trilling and was doing

acrobatics on its swing. Imperceptibly, Desmond led the conversation in the direction of the Blakes. The Morrows could tell him very little except, approvingly, that the couple were apparently content with each other's company—"So many people these days seem to have a dread of being alone"—and there was very little coming and going in the evenings. They had no idea what Emmett Blake did for a living; they had gathered that Mrs. Blake worked at an advertising agency but didn't know whether or not her job ever took her out of Boston.

They did clear up what had been a point of interest to Desmond and now fell flat. "Such *impulsive* people," said Mrs. Morrow tolerantly. "We'd known they were moving, of course, that gets around a building like this at once, but it was supposed to be on the second of January. We'd had a very mild Christmas, almost soupy, in fact, and I happened to meet Mrs. Blake in the lobby in the afternoon and she said something about Currier and Ives spinning in their graves and they were going to move right away as there was no reason why not. And they did."

It had the ring of authenticity, although Desmond would have described Paula Blake as impatient rather than impulsive. Still, nothing made present surroundings pall like the fact of new surroundings simply waiting to be occupied, and when you threw in a warmish Christmas—

"I understand the Nicholsons came to say good-bye," said Desmond casually, "and maybe got roped into helping with the moving."

But that dating had been either forgetfulness or pure spite on the superintendent's part, because Mrs. Morrow said at once, "Oh, no, they were last here—at least that we knew of—a few days before Christmas. I remember it particularly because it was the night you went to bed early with that awful cold, Harold"—side glance at her husband, who nodded judiciously like a man who kept card indexes of his colds—"and I was still up addressing a few last-minute Christmas cards, and I heard a man's voice in the hall saying, 'Naomi, tell Philip he can have another drink'—that was Mr. Blake—and the other man said they had to drive all the way to Wrexley."

Philip Nicholson, in Wrexley.

Desmond thanked the Morrows, more deeply than they realized, and they were the honest people they had seemed. When, mindful of boastful friends with parakeets, he asked at the door if their bird talked at all, Mrs. Morrow said apologetically, "Well, no. It said something that sounded vaguely like hello when we bought it, but it's even forgotten that."

Boston had been face-lifted since Desmond's last visit, but a restaurant he liked was still in its proper place. Tomorrow he would telephone Mrs. Nicholson, pose as an old friend who had been out of touch, find out her husband's office. If he couldn't inveigle Nicholson to lunch he would ask to see the other man for a few minutes on business, describe Paula Blake, and inquire about New Orleans. Man to man, he would be; he might even go against his principles and wink.

The trouble with all this was that if he and Duffy hadn't been sober, the chances were that Nicholson hadn't been either. Confronted by an unremembered face bearing an unremembered name, he would advise Desmond Moran to get the hell out of there. Even if he did remember, he might very well do the same thing.

People did not as a rule take kindly to probings into their personal pasts.

Still, it was a thread-end which Desmond could not relinquish. Paula Blake had lied about New Orleans; together with her husband she had made every effort to keep Mrs. Chilton at arm's length—odd in a to them new and fairly isolated spot; not long after leaving the Blake house, Mrs. Chilton was dead. To a fellow smoker, the virginally white clamshell ash tray, which had not only been flushed out by a hose but stepped crunchingly on by a fireman later, was as suspect as bones in a vegetarian's garbage pail.

Mrs. Chilton might well have required a second sleeping pill, which the autopsy had indicated, after the quarrel with her daughter which Desmond had clearly walked in upon. But it was as reasonable to argue extra caution on her part as well as extra carelessness: as a frequent user of them, she would be familiar with the effects of sleeping pills. It seemed such a very pat and explicable way for her to die; if her own daughter accepted it—indeed with a strong undertone of "I told her so"—who else would raise a question? If he had not seen that unmarked white shell with its neat little huddle of cigarette butts, Desmond would have been shocked but not incredulous.

On the way back to his hotel, ludicrous paraphrases of "Who was that lady I saw you with three years ago?" went through his head. Strain though he would, Desmond could not recall Nicholson's having introduced him to Paula Blake; she had simply been there with him and, later, there had been some kind of talk . . .

Incongruously, or perhaps very congruously, it was Lydia Peel who occupied Desmond's mind as he was falling asleep. She had the bewitching Donahue eyes, fringed in her case with gold-tipped lashes almost thick enough to paint with, but he suspected that she was not quite as uncomplicated as the rest of that likable clan. She responded like litmus paper, and she was seeing the Blakes tonight. Just as well, decidedly, that she had believed him in his rationalization of Mrs. Chilton's death.

In the morning, it took him less than sixty seconds to learn from the operator, with a flourish, that the telephone for Philip A. Nicholson, 5 Garden Circle, Wrexley, was no longer in service.

Philip could be a middle name, Desmond reminded himself, furiously unwilling for his bird to be flown; he knew one P. R. Palmer who was never called anything but Bob. Further consultance with the operator, however, produced no Nicholson with P. as a middle initial. Could she tell him when the number had last been in service? No, she could not. With a morose look at the weather, which as on previous visits to Boston looked capable of mildewing anyone who stayed out in it long, Desmond packed his bag, settled his bill, and at the desk inquired the easiest way to Wrexley.

In the cab on the way to the station, he felt an unreasonable disappointment at not having heard from the Morrows. Conscious of something left unsaid or unclarified during that interview last night, he had given them his number at the hotel and also in Elder's Farms. They were obviously scrupulous and well-intentioned people, and if they had not thought of anything to add to their disclosures by 9 A.M. the next day, chances were that they never would.

* * *

Like most people in their age group, the Morrows dieted carefully during the week. They undid it all on Saturday mornings, when the apartment was fragrant with sausage, fried eggs, English muffins and coffee. Over this repast Mrs. Morrow said at shortly before nine o'clock, "I do think we ought to let him know, Harold. It mightn't be important, but he seemed so interested and he's gone away with a wrong impression."

Mr. Morrow had his pipe out again. Morning had brought caution. "Do you think he was here on behalf of his brother, really?"

"I doubt if he even has a brother," said his wife urbanely, "but he was a very nice man. I liked him. For one thing, he took an interest in Davy. I made a note of his telephone number on the margin of the—"

They gazed at each other in instant dismay. In the intervals between scratch paper on the floor of the parakeet's cage, it was Mr. Morrow's habit to use newspaper lining, taking the first section at hand. As they always folded their newspaper after reading it as neatly as though they were passing it along, it was the first section on which Mrs. Morrow had made her notation. And Davy, bouncing and clawing and pecking with energy, had reduced it to a miniature snowdrift.

Chapter 9

It was not, thought Lydia with surprising sadness, a day on which to be buried. The morning was full of splashes and sparkles as the snow melted under a sun of such brilliance that, occasionally, refracted light trembled along the living-room walls. There was an almost brook-like music from the eaves, and now and then a feathery plop as a branch released its burden.

She was no fonder of funerals than the Blakes, but she would have felt somehow bound even without Candide's pointed instructions; there were people who poked through their outer fabric and touched you on rare occasions, and Mrs. Chilton had been one of them. Still, it came as a relief when Candide telephoned to say that Laura, her baby-sitter, had called up sick.

"—not that I believe a word of it. I know for a fact that she has some pathetic little boyfriend going back to the Navy, but of *all* days it leaves me with Harry, so could you possibly come and stay with him? He's a bit young for funerals, I feel, and I simply don't know who else to ask. I could send a cab for you so that you don't have to drive through all this slop."

Lydia gazed through the dining-room window at the flashing confrontation of sun and snow. "I don't mind driving at all, but under the circumstances, mightn't Harry feel better with someone he's more used to? He seems to like Mrs. Telfair."

"They're going to the funeral," said Candide with a kind of mad logic, "and although they have a housekeeper, of course, they also have a cat. Harry has a thing about cats—they tend to tease him and naturally, being so young, he retaliates. Aelurophiles simply cannot understand."

Lydia had a briefly entertained vision of cats, who sensibly fled at the approach of small children, coming out to tease Harry. Poking him with their paws, perhaps, and then running coyly away? And—dawningly—this was why Candide had had to deposit Harry with her the other afternoon. He had done something horrible to the Telfairs' cat in the course of his overnight stay and been ruled off the premises, and—the memory of secret activity in the living room when she came back from the kitchen with his ginger ale returned—he had been peering under the chairs and couches to see if *she* had a cat.

Still, staying with him was preferable to going to the funeral, by a hair, and Candide had sounded as though she really had no other choice. Lydia said, "Ten-fifteen or thereabouts, to be on the safe side?" and Candide said yes, and she would give her a cup of coffee. Her voice came over the wire a little blurred, as if grief had finally caught up with her. Well, it would be grim to be alone on this of all occasions. Lydia wondered fleetingly at Jones Haviland for leaving her, and then realized that this was, all things considered, an ideal time for him to be off the scene.

The Donahues had the local paper delivered, and a photograph on the front page below the fold showed a fuzzy Mrs. Chilton wearing dark lipstick and a 1940's hat. The cause of death was given as "smoke inhalation resulting from a fire at her home," and a summing-up followed of the career of her late photographer husband. All of it seemed alien to the forthright and beaky-nosed woman who had wondered why the Surgeon General didn't speak up about cigarette holes in clothes, and asked about the "marvelous digs" in New Mexico.

An ancient car, being driven as though it were already part of the funeral procession, turned out of the Chilton driveway as Lydia entered it. A vague impression of familiarity, something to do with the driver's head, sharpened into the fact of an outsize beret: the self-declared writer or artist whom she had seen in the liquor store. Moments later, Candide confirmed this.

"You're an angel to come, Lydia. I've just gotten rid of Arthur Dunsworth—do you remember him at all? I daresay he's a character, but he's also a trial and a bore and he and Mother fought like cats and dogs. Would you like a cup of coffee? Harry, stand up and say hello to Miss Peel."

Harry, today wearing gray flannel shorts, stood up and sat down again with a jack-in-the-box effect, saying nothing at all. Lydia glanced around her, not as he and Jones Haviland had but for a swift general impression. The living room was big and airily windowed, and because of its very size the unmatched chintzes, apricot and gold, blue and green and rose, did not fight but got along together with a curiously pleasant effect. As Paula Blake had said, everything was contemporary, except for a walnut chest carved with clustered grapes and leaves. It looked Jacobean. Lydia commented on it and Candide said, leading the way to the kitchen, "That is rather nice, isn't it? It was Simon Wister's—he knew Mother adored it and left it to her in his will."

Lydia would have imagined Mrs. Chilton pottering comfortably about in a country kitchen, but here there was a long sweep of formica counter with double steel sinks, a sophisticated oven, a refrigerator large enough to keep people in if necessary. Apparently not having heard her earlier "No, thanks," Candide poured a cup of coffee from an imposing glass contraption and said baldly, "Harrison is here, at the inn. He came for the funeral."

"That was nice of him," said Lydia, and earned herself an angry, slaty stare.

"Nice!" Candide slapped the coffeemaker down with dangerous force. "He's probably here to see if he can find grounds for upsetting the custody—not that Mother didn't make a pet of him."

It wasn't grief which had affected her voice on the telephone, thought Lydia with detachment; it was resentment and fear that someone, out of malice or sheer clumsiness, would mention Jones Haviland. Why had she ever supposed Candide capable of an emotion not related to her own well-being?

She said with a faint crispness, "I have a notion that your mother was very much liked here. For that reason alone I can't imagine people trying to stir up trouble, today of all days."

"Well . . ." said Candide with an unconvinced air, and threw a distracted glance at the clock. "I'd better be getting ready to leave. Harry will amuse himself but I'd rather he didn't go outside, he'll simply track mud in. He likes to cut pictures out of magazines—the only thing is that he's sometimes a bit careless with the scissors. His lunch can wait until I get back, or there are graham crackers . . . and do, *do* make yourself a drink at some appropriate time." She waved an indicative hand, managing to invest this gesture with the assurance, after close study, that Lydia could be trusted with the liquor cabinet. "There's practically everything, under there."

In the living room, she buttoned herself into the chestnut cape, placed the webbiest of black mantillas over her pale hair, pulled on fawn kid gloves, said to Harry, "Darling, fetch me Grandmama's black prayer book, it's on the shelf of the bedside table in her room," and, astonishingly, gave Lydia a faint down-turned smile. "Lucky it survived, isn't it? I'm afraid I'm not similarly equipped."

There was a joke which said, "Before they made you, they threw away the mold." Harry came back with the prayer book, and not a minute too soon: a long black limousine had slid past the front windows. It already held two occupants—Mrs. Chilton's lawyer and his wife, Lydia learned later, and friends for twenty years—and Candide departed in a discreet whiff of scent and she was alone with Harry.

Apart from a single baleful glance at her when the door closed, Harry appeared unaware of her presence—except, Lydia noted, that his page-turning picked up tempo. She was amused and a little touched to see that he was holding a copy of *Vogue;* the long-necked model on the cover, who looked somewhat as though she had uncoiled out of a basket in answer to the playing of a pipe, wasn't unlike Candide. Since his opening of Mrs. Chilton's bedroom door, there was a faint bitter suggestion of smoke on the air.

Lydia was content with silence until Harry chose to

break it. She finished her coffee, which in spite of its expensive provenance was not as good as her own instant brand, lit a cigarette, reached for an oversized book on the coffee table. It was a biography of Schliemann, more for lay readers than fellow archeologists, as the back contained a section of photographed sites which had yielded modest finds to amateur diggers. There was a loop of ink drawn around—

"You're not the boss of me," said Harry militantly from behind his drawn-up knees.

"No," agreed Lydia, and he was so surprised that it took him seconds to rearrange his mouth, which had been open for further defiance.

"This is *my* house," he announced dangerously after a small interval.

"It's very nice, too." Was there actually a struggle for the custody of this child? Might as well deal with him on his own naked terms. "Did you ever get your grandmother's shovel?" inquired Lydia.

Harry shook his silky mop of hair and scowled, as though this failure might have been her fault.

"Well, no doubt you'll have one of your own someday. Where did your grandmother dig?" asked Lydia curiously. It was a measure of his apparently total imperviousness that she felt no compunction at putting questions in this vein.

Harry gave her a haughty look and transferred his gaze to the wall above her head. His attitude said that this was no proper concern of hers; even on such short acquaintance, Lydia suspected that he didn't know and didn't want to admit it. After a moment she picked up the book again and returned to the page with the inked circle. The caption said that the site was in Arizona, but something about the contours looked familiar. She was puzzling mildly over this when the telephone rang.

Harry flashed off the couch and across the room. He picked up the telephone in the middle of the second ring, answered in his usual fashion, and pressed the receiver closer to his ear in a baffled way, breathing audibly and hopefully into the mouthpiece before he replaced it. "They hung up," he said, disappointed.

Someone mis-dialing, and not bothering to apologize. Or someone reading in the newspaper the time of the funeral and testing to see if the house was empty? This was not New York or Detroit or even Albuquerque, Lydia told herself, but she took her coffee cup out to the kitchen, washed it, and locked the door there.

Something fast and furtive was going on in the living room. There was the slide of wood, a chinking sound of metal and, just as Lydia reached the doorway, the crash as the drawer of the telephone table—a forbidden place, obviously, from the speed with which Harry had taken advantage of her brief absence—hit the floor. A flashlight and extra batteries and a number of keys rolled and bounced, but there had been a single sharp crack on impact.

Harry had heard it too; he watched with a breath-holding air while Lydia retrieved the drawer, pressed the laterally shivered side together and managed to jockey it back into its grooves. As he knelt to help gather up the fallen objects, he said anxiously, "Don't tell Mummy," and Lydia, struck by this evidence of normalcy, assured him that she would not.

While Harry half-disappeared under a chair in search of a flashlight battery, she picked up keys, some tagged, some evidently familiar enough to need no labeling. A neatly printed "Wister" took her by surprise until she remembered Mrs. Chilton's mention of a warning or two before the fatal heart attack. In this fairly remote area, Simon Wister would have liked a good friend to have access to his house in case of emergency.

Barring dearly loved relatives or the closest of friends, no one would care for the thought that a key to his house existed in other hands, but Lydia had to shut firmly out of her mind the Blakes' reaction if they knew. And why had Paula lied about "parting" with the carved chest? Because she had to seize on the first explanation, no matter how shaky, to cover the real reason for her husband's furious mood?

When Lydia thought it must be at least two o'clock, and Candide had been taken off to a long restorative lunch, it was not quite twelve. To kill time, although Harry gave no indication of being hungry as he wielded his scissors dangerously close to the couch cover, she proposed getting him some lunch.

Candide was either planning to shop later in the day or depart from Elder's Farms. The refrigerator offered a shaven lemon, a single strip of bacon, a promising but empty egg carton, an inch of butter, a pint of milk, and a half-empty jar of pickled asparagus. (That was probably Harry's.) The pantry wasn't much better stocked, but there were saltines and Lydia found, offered and heated a can of tomato soup.

Why, it occurred to her for the first time, had Candide, who had never pretended any real grief, been visiting her mother at all? The answer came back with speed: to be near Jones Haviland under circumstances of the utmost respectability. Mrs. Chilton hadn't approved, the painter had said he was anathema . . .

It was almost one o'clock when Candide returned with the lawyer and his wife, who would be disappointed indeed if they were expecting funeral baked meats. Lydia said no to a drink, proposed a little as though it were a baby-sitting fee, and Candide went with her to the door. "I didn't see Desmond Moran there," she remarked peevishly, "which seems a trifle odd, all things considered."

"Oh, he's out of town," said Lydia with an air of casual, didn't-you-know surprise, and nursed a childish pleasure all the way to her car.

The pay telephone outside the service station which the Blakes used had evidently been repaired; the door of the booth was open and Lydia, halted at a red light, saw Paula Blake inside, running a finger down a page of the directory. She must have been wearing her hair differently; it took Lydia a moment to recognize her. With the camera in its usual place beside her, it would save a lot of driving if she could take her pictures now instead of coming back at three—but the tiny delay spoiled that. The booth door closed, the light changed, a car behind Lydia honked imperatively.

Perhaps because it had somewhat the guise of a business appointment, perhaps because the memory of her first arrival was still sharp, she did not look forward to her afternoon mission; although the photographs were for Susan, she would be there on sufferance. Over a glass of cold Chablis which she considered she had well and truly earned, Lydia tried to analyze the ambivalence of her own feelings toward the Blakes.

When she was with them she liked them—Emmett more than the tense and concentrated Paula, in fact; it was only in retrospect that there was something almost disturbing about the solidarity between husband and wife. The closest comparison Lydia could make was her first day at a new school, when all the other children, temporarily forgetting their differences, had seemed to know something she didn't and were faintly malicious about it. Certainly they had aroused Desmond's curiosity. Was that what had taken him out of Elder's Farms?

Lydia felt an undefined alarm at the thought; it was as though by bringing the Colonial mirror she had become an unwitting participant in something she would just as soon not know about. At twenty minutes of three, with the unreal feeling that she was four days back in time, she set out again for Violet Lane.

Chapter 10

Emmett Blake's memory was evidently as clear as Lydia's; he called a greeting from the open front door as she got out of the Volvo with her camera. "Where are the snows of yesteryear? Come on in—Paula's upstairs getting beautiful but she'll be right down."

Lydia followed him into the blue and white living room where Mrs. Chilton had sat so recently in her tweeds and sturdy shoes. The mirror, holding the reflected iridescence of a luster vase, had the air of belonging exactly between two organdy-curtained windows, and she said so. Emmett looked pleased, and eyed her camera. "Just like ours, so I suppose there's no chance of an indoor shot. Have you ever noticed that all the really expensive cameras are in the hands of people with beards and patches?"

There was a brisk clatter of heels on the stairs and Paula came in, wearing a topaz-colored pants suit over a ribbed cream shell. "Look at me, all got up for the photographer. It's awfully nice of you to take this trouble, Lydia, particularly on top of a funeral. How was it, by the way, apart from ghastly?"

"I didn't go," said Lydia, and explained why. It crossed her mind as she spoke that people who wore glasses, and especially shell-rimmed ones, looked more alert than other people, as though they were utilizing their vision to the fullest. "As a matter of fact, I nearly stopped on my way home—I saw you at the corner telephone—but I had traffic behind me."

The front door had apparently swelled with moisture, and Paula gave it a wrench. "Too bad you didn't—I'd gotten stuck and Emmett knocked off early too . . . What a gorgeous day!"

It was. The combination of melting snow and sun had brought new green to clear patches on the tiny front lawn, and the wood of the apple trees was faintly flushed. The eaves dripped with a measured and timeless sound. "Darling, your collar's turned up in back—there," said Paula, and, to Lydia, "By the front door, like this?"

Lydia backed off and examined them through the view finder. The simplest of cameras afflicted her with a dread conviction that she was going to cut off people's heads or feet, or put a finger in the way or tilt the camera and produce a seasick slant. Very often she had been proved right. Emmett and Paula smiled confidently back at her without being glassy and bulge-eyed about it, and she took two shots and then retreated for one of the house itself, small and pewtery in the clasp of apple-tree shadows.

"You must come in and have a glass of Madeira so we won't be drinking alone," said Paula when this had been accomplished. "Besides, I want to show you something."

In the house, she vanished upstairs while Emmett poured Madeira, returning with an unframed canvas which she propped against the back of the couch. "Emmett did this last winter of our parents' old summer place on Cape Cod. I haven't the faintest notion of what Susan's house is like—do you think she'd want this for her birthday?"

The painting had a spellbinding quality. Through a delicate close-up of gray—bayberries? beach plums?—snow swept away downhill to a chimneyed and glowing red house, occupying no more than a square inch of canvas but drawing the eye like a jewel nestled in icy white velvet. The effect was of a radiance so compelling that you were willing to go out in the frozen stillness to reach it.

"It's stunning," said Lydia honestly, looking for and finding Emmett's signature meshed in with the gray. "She's told me about the house. I think she'd love it."

Emmett put in the predictable demurrer that there was too much blue in his snow. Paula said contentedly, "Good. There's lots of time, of course, but I'm glad we thought of it."

Lots of time was putting it mildly, thought Lydia, glancing over the rim of her wine glass; Susan had had a birthday in December. She remembered it very well because Susan, still unsure of herself with Miles, had asked that Lydia and one of Santa Fe's most eligible and slippery bachelors come to dinner too, and they had gotten stuck in the snow on Canyon Road. (Brandy having followed champagne, the bachelor had telephoned Lydia at an unconscionable hour the next morning to try and discover in a circuitous way if he had been, er, talkative? "You're teasing, my dearest," Lydia had answered, to pay him back for waking her up so early. "You can't have forgotten about the special license and the sapphire mink . . . oh, relax, Dick, all you said was good night.")

"Incidentally, we called Susan last night—we

couldn't bear the suspense," Paula was saying now. "I must say I could have saved my breath, not to speak of three dollars plus. I suppose Miles Marsh was there. Anyway, she was terribly cheery and airy, as though there were no momentous decisions at all. She was going away for the weekend, she said"—Paula cast a mildly inquiring glance at Lydia—"and she'd write as soon as she got back. That was it, period."

Confined to the gallery as she was during the week, Susan often deputized her assistant on Saturdays and visited friends in Espanola or Taos. Before Lydia could formulate any further thought, Emmett said with a wry smile, "We weren't all that forthcoming with our own announcement, as I remember. I'd say Susan has a perfect right."

Paula colored for the first time in Lydia's observation, the flush turning her eyes to lime. "Well, but Susan's wedding was yards of satin and lace and all the trimmings. We both agreed that we couldn't ask her to cross the country by train for our tiny little informal ceremony."

But a sister would certainly have liked an option, thought Lydia. Had Susan suspected, and was there any accuracy in the suspicion, that at the time they hadn't considered her stable enough to attend a wedding? Small wonder, in that case, that Emmett wasn't represented in Susan's gallery; a thing like that might be understood and forgiven but never entirely forgotten. Something sharply personal had entered the room. Emmett rose, poured more wine into Lydia's glass before she could stop him, said lightly, "Is it water over the dam or under the bridge? I can never remember. I don't know why we're visiting all this on your head, Lydia. How long are you staying, by the way?"

Only until the day after next, Lydia told him. The words sounded strange to her as she said them; at the moment, this moist, wooded, cloud-churned country seemed the only reality and Santa Fe a long sunny dream. In answer to a further question from Paula—another layer of gloss over that brief awkwardness?—she explained that, having spent her summers almost exclusively at the beach with her clannish cousins, she had no old friends to look up.

"Of course I've seen people who look familiar, in town, but I can see that they're having the same trouble with me, so we just smile vaguely, in case, and go on our way. The only person I've talked to, apart from you"—deliberately she did not mention Desmond Moran, so alertly interested in these people—"is Candide Blackwood, and that's been more or less in the line of duty."

And now, surely, having passed and re-passed the chair where she had sat, one of the Blakes would remark that the last time Lydia had been here so had Mrs. Chilton—but Paula remarked instead that Emmett had encountered the same almost-recognition from a few people when they first moved to Elder's Farms. "Which is really amazing, considering that he was eighteen—weren't you, darling?—and only here for a couple of weeks . . ."

This was polite small talk, and Lydia finished her Madeira and rose. There was the usual slow progress to the door on such occasions: thank you for the wine and that nice dinner; thank *you* for the mirror carrying and picture taking; have a good trip back and best love to Susan. Lydia turned the Volvo, waved back to the waving pair in the doorway, and drove out past the knoll. For some reason, and not to do with the wine, she found herself peculiarly bemused.

*   *   *

Paula poured herself more Madeira. "You may not have noticed," she said, "but she kept looking at me." Her voice was very calm.

Emmett cast a keen glance at her glass and refilled his own. "I don't follow."

Paula enlightened him, adding irritably, "And don't start whistling, because it won't help."

A kind of tense concentration began to filter into the room, almost as detectable as perfume or mist. "No," said Emmett, thoughtful. "No. *But* . . ."

Because of the Nicholsons' connection with the fastidious Blakes, Garden Circle in Wrexley was a surprise to Desmond Moran. An untended-looking necklace of yellowish imitation-brick duplexes, it needed trees the way a woman with a bad figure needed well-designed clothes, but apart from a few of the grim sharp-bladed evergreens that tended to sprout around mortuaries, there weren't any. A realtor's For Rent sign was planted in the tiny brownish lawn of 5 A.

A loud party seemed to be in progress at 5 B, although it wasn't quite noon, and Desmond knocked twice before the door swung warily in on the length of its chain. After a glance at the bright brown no-nonsense eye of a woman in a dark blue bathrobe, he decided to tell no elaborate lies but said, after giving his name, that he had hoped to find the Nicholsons.

A sudden sharp gust of wind came to his assistance. The woman—Avis Tuttle, she told him presently—shivered and took the door off its chain. "You'd better come in before I catch pneumonia. I hope you've had the flu."

Desmond said falsely that he had. The small living

room reeked so strongly of liniment that his eyes began to water when the front door had closed. The party sounds emanated from a game show on a color television screen, featuring cerise-faced contestants wearing chartreuse clothing. Miss Tuttle gave it a wistful look but turned the set off, invited Desmond to sit down, and, plump and ruddy-skinned in spite of her illness, settled herself in a chair. She said in a forthright tone, "I hope it's nothing important, because you're nearly three months late. The Nicholsons moved out just before Christmas."

So Christmas was a focal point—but of what? Had the Blakes' impending departure triggered the Nicholsons', or was it the other way around? Coincidence could certainly be dismissed, thought Desmond, and stared so brilliantly at Miss Tuttle without seeing her that she shifted in her chair, sending a new whiff of liniment his way, and said, "Christmas Day, in fact. It seemed such an awkward time for moving. I didn't even know they were gone until the next morning."

The classic moonlight flit? Miss Tuttle, interpreting Desmond's puzzlement correctly, explained that she was a nurse on the four-to-midnight shift at the South Shore Hospital and as a consequence had scarcely seen the Nicholsons since she had taken the apartment the previous September. "She worked too, which was a blessing because after they left in the mornings I could go back to sleep—these walls are like paper," explained Miss Tuttle.

"Strange that they didn't mention it over the weekend, in case you had a friend who was looking for an apartment," said Desmond. It occurred to him that they were discussing the Nicholsons quite openly; the nurse still retained some curiosity about the nearly invisible neighbors who had departed with such abruptness.

"I'm never here on the weekends. I go to my sister's —she's got a houseful of kids, and after looking at patients all week, it makes a nice change. Maybe," said Miss Tuttle, "they got right out of this climate, the Southwest or somewhere, what with him being so sick in November."

Desmond gazed at her, entranced. He took out his cigarettes, asking automatically if she minded, and when she said with astonishing cordiality that yes, she did, he put them away again, wishing briefly that he could deprive her of her liniment and tissues. "What was the matter with him, do you know?"

"Pneumonia," said Miss Tuttle with a trace of professional pride. "He was in the hospital for ten days, not on my floor, but I asked one of the other girls and he had a bad reaction to the antibiotics. His wife must certainly have been worried, because she didn't come home the whole time."

"They must be a very devoted couple."

"Well, there's nothing like a serious illness to bring out devotion," said Miss Tuttle practically, "but I will say they were a quiet pair—usually asleep, you know, by the time I got home from work." An eerie echo of something floated through Desmond's mind, and was destroyed when the nurse said dryly, "You can't quarrel privately in these apartments. The only time—excuse me a minute."

She vanished, apparently to apply a fresh embrocation; when she came back Desmond's barely recovered nasal passages began to sting fierily all over again. She did not resume her chair, and it took him a moment to realize that she wasn't going to. In that short absence she had been seized by some kind of compunction about discussing a former patient of the hospital's—or the absence had been a pretext for forgetting whatever she had been about to say.

"My bursitis—I suppose everybody has a point of least resistance, don't they?" she said, massaging her shoulder. "I must get over it by Monday, as we're short-handed. I'm sorry I haven't been able to help you."

With no choice, possessed by a furious sense of frustration, Desmond got to his feet. "But I think you can. For security reasons," he managed to invest this ancient phrase with dignity, "I can't tell you why it's so important that the Nicholsons be located, but anything you can tell me about them might be vital. And would be confidential."

Now, he thought, holding her gaze severely, Miss Tuttle would ask for some kind of credentials—but apparently she was at her best telling patients commandingly that they could not get up or that they must get up. She said, toying with her sash in a mesmerized way, "Well, it was nothing, really, just that a few days before they moved out they came home very late—I was just getting to sleep—and it was the only time I'd heard them have anything like an argument. Mrs. Nicholson seemed to want to go somewhere, it would be well worth the trip, she said, and he said something like "Are you out of your mind?' and they went back and forth about it."

A faint cold prickle, this time nothing to do with the liniment, touched Desmond. "Did either of them mention a place called Elder's Farms?"

Miss Tuttle had no idea. "I cannot do without my

sleep," she said firmly, "so I put in my ear stopples."

Ear stopples. As simple as that, when otherwise she could probably have unraveled the whole tangle. Desmond thanked her, hoped her bursitis would be better, and, hand on the doorknob, inquired about the Nicholsons' car. An old gray Volkswagen, Miss Tuttle told him, and it was his turn for compunction: her face showed the beginnings of worry. "I live alone, as you see, so whatever this is about, I certainly hope my name won't come into it."

Desmond assured her that it would not, and added that in any case the Nicholsons would be grateful when he located them. On this unlikely note he left, pausing on the doorstep to light the cigarette forbidden inside. An under-twenty couple emerged from the next duplex, hand in hand, identically blue-jeaned and jacketed, the girl with glasses and long straight hair, the boy with glasses and a beard. They were bound for their mailbox. On the premise that answers were sometimes found in unlikely places, Desmond called, "I'm looking for the Nicholsons, who used to live in Five A—would you have any idea of where they moved to?"

They gazed at him as blankly as if he had posed some question about dinosaurs. The boy resumed whatever he had been saying; the girl, either more polite or less uncivil, tossed over her shoulder, "We didn't know them. Sorry."

So much for answers in unlikely places. Desmond had taken a cab from the station, but it wasn't much over a mile and he walked back; there wasn't a train to South Station for nearly an hour, in any case. A bone-biting wind made him feel as if Miss Tuttle's flu-turned-bursitis were already at work, although he knew it to be clinically impossible.

He thought about his rough timetable of events. Nicholson hospitalized in November, his devoted wife presumably renting a room to be frequently at his side. Both of them visiting the Blakes several days before Christmas and subsequently—this was a guess, but their late return had stood out in the nurse's memory—arguing about a trip somewhere. The Blakes deciding quixotically to take possession of the Elder's Farms house immediately after Christmas instead of January second as scheduled.

Had they, Desmond wondered, informed the Nicholsons about the change in plans?

On the heels of that came another speculation, so wild that if he had not had time on his hands he might have dismissed it outright. But the telephone booth at the station was vacant, a circumstance that came about so rarely for him that it might have been an omen, and the local directory dangled invitingly. He dialed Miss Tuttle's number, apologized for disturbing her again, and put a single question. Clearly relieved at something that could not be regarded as gossip, she gave him the answer at once.

He had thought, before, in terms of a thread-end which he could not relinquish. He thought now in terms of fine and nearly invisible wire leading to what, under its look of quiescence, might just possibly be a freshly armed bomb.

Chapter II

With the kind of timing to be expected, the telephone which had been ringing while Lydia's cold-numbed fingers struggled with the door key fell silent just before she reached it. Instead of dissipating at once, the echoes seemed to leave holes in the always dubious silence of an empty house re-entered after a span of time: too complete, too innocent, as if someone, just before leaving, had spoken menacingly to the refrigerator, the oil burner, all the producers of tiny house sounds.

"Whoever it was will call again," said Lydia aloud, to break the utter stillness, and went boldly into the kitchen to put on the kettle for a cup of tea.

It was after four-thirty because, heartened by the camera's earlier docility, she had stopped on her way home to photograph catkins spearing out of a tiny pond set in a ruffle of snow; with its background of firs it would make a diverting wall scene for a New Mexico summer. At some point between pond and house the weather had changed with the effect of a cosmic finger-snap, the temperature dropping so sharply that bushes were caught in surprised attitudes and, here and there, tree branches were laced together with what looked like polished cobwebs.

It was faintly depressing that she had very possibly discovered the site of Mrs. Chilton's digging.

Lydia's first arrival at the Blakes' had shown her only the close façade of shingles and small-paned windows shuttered in blue set among apple trees. Her retreat a little way up the knoll to get all of the house on film for Susan had given her a longer perspective, the view finder roaming briefly over a patch of disturbed earth, points of soil poking through the snow, just in front of a low stone wall that enclosed most of the orchard. The patch ran out of sight behind the north wall of the house, where Emmett would do his painting. Even if this had been April instead of an inclement period of March, it could scarcely be preparations for a border; what would grow in the deep shade of the apple trees?

According to Mrs. Chilton, Simon Wister had once found a piece of pewter on his property—in that area? But a request for an extension of her digging could not have sent Emmett into his controlled fury when all he had to say was no.

Edgily, Lydia made her tea. Given the circumstance, she would have said practically to someone else, "Why didn't you ask them outright? Or say, 'I see you've gotten an early start on your garden'? They'd have had to answer you one way or another."

Why not, indeed? Was it because—Lydia tried to reduce her own feeling to comprehensible terms—there was something very slightly daunting about the Blakes? Paula, whose glasses only added to her look of acuity, and even Emmett with all his urbanity? They were friendly, in fact with an almost burning-glass focus—but Lydia found herself thinking that so was a paring knife friendly, if you were in a position of having to peel potatoes, until you made a wrong move and it turned and bit you across the palm.

Nonsense. The Blakes hadn't mentioned Mrs. Chilton apart from a blithe inquiry about the funeral because they hadn't really liked her and refused to make a hypocritical parade of sorrow, although there were times, undeniably, when hypocrisy was soothing. Lydia took an absent and scalding sip of tea, put the cup down hastily, glanced back over the last few seconds of thought. Something puzzlingly wrong, there . . . and the telephone was ringing again.

She had been half-expecting it to be Desmond, and was taken aback by the high-pitched voice which belonged to Jones Haviland, in Marblehead. He said he had been trying to reach Candide ever since three; was she at Lydia's?

"No, I haven't seen her since she got back from the funeral."

For the second time, Lydia explained her sojourn with Harry at the Chilton house. Haviland agreed that it had been wise to spare the child what he called "those savage rites," but seemed to feel that Lydia should have remained on the scene—perhaps to see that Candide put her feet up, pat her hand occasionally, bring her restoratives? "I really don't think you need worry about Candide," said Lydia, turning to contemplate the leaf-cracked mirror. "She's bearing up very well."

"She's wonderfully courageous. Look, I'm going to be away from a telephone for the next couple of hours, but I must get a message to her as soon as possible—may I leave it with you?"

"Well . . . yes," said Lydia with reluctance. She hated responsibilities like this, passed on so airily by the giver, assuming the weight of boulders for the middle man. "All I can do is try the house, though."

"Tell her," said Haviland, firm and unheeding, "that she's *not* to leave Elder's Farms tonight, and that I'll call her later on."

Lydia, remembering the state of Mrs. Chilton's refrigerator, suspected that this message was not going to be received with any particular glee. *If* she could be reached, if she and Harry weren't already on their way to—Marblehead, was the implication. Lydia tried the Chilton number without success, took a very hot bath because she was still cold, wondered, as she soaked, about Susan. Either the evening had not turned out as Susan thought, or she had mentioned the idea of the art-student-watcher to Miles and that had somehow sparked off difficulties. I should have shut my eyes to the whole business, Lydia told herself, staring at the ceiling—but then what about the almost inevitable time when Miles was caught and charged, in an essentially close-knit community like Santa Fe?

And she had forgotten all about calling Candide. Lydia sprang out of her bath and into a long robe, listened to the empty ringing at the Chilton house, and after a moment of indecision called Desmond Moran's number. He was in a position to see when the lights went on in the other house, signaling Candide's return, and although it was clear that he knew all about Jones Haviland, Lydia would go through the charade of asking him to let Candide know that she had a message for her.

The phone burred once. A prim voice piped, "Mrs. Chilton's residence," and in the background a woman said amusedly, "Darling, we aren't at home."

"Hello, Harry," said Lydia. He was everywhere, she thought, like flu. "This is Lydia Peel. May I speak to your mother?"

Harry, taken aback by his error, breathed wordlessly into her ear for a few seconds; then, after a distant and uninformative "Mummy," Candide's crisp imperious voice said, "Yes?"

The single syllable, addressed as to yet another telephone solicitor, made Lydia bristle. She delivered Jones Haviland's message with matching crispness and a certain satisfaction, and there was a displeased little silence at the other end of the line. "Well, but there must have been more to it than that. I mean"—Candide gave a small unentertained laugh—"a reason."

"That was it in its entirety," Lydia told her pleasantly.

"Oh. What a bore, but thank you anyway, Lydia. Wait, hold on a second . . ."

"I tried to get you a little while ago," said Desmond Moran's voice, as brisk as though they were picking up an earlier conversation. "We're waiting for Candide's garage to let her know if her car is ready—"

("Someone told me you were good with cars.")

"—but that should be any minute. I wondered if you were free for dinner?"

Lydia said she was and would like it very much. When she had hung up she found herself, no doubt because of that echo from ten years ago, approaching something she thought she had long outgrown: a near-fluster. She had let her hair get wet at the ends in her bath, and it had dried in soft feathery points instead of its usual disciplined fall. She had traveled light to Elder's Farms, and although fashion magazines were lyrical about the transforming effect of accessories on that *good* dress you had already been seen in twice, to Lydia it looked like the identical dress with a twist of chiffon which would not stay anchored no matter how she dealt with it, and gold earrings instead of pearl. Feeling that something more in the innovation was called for, she darkened the tips of her eyelashes.

All this had lost her most of the five o'clock news. What remained of it was a denture-adhesive commercial (the successful user bared her teeth at an apple like a latter-day vampire), then what had the exciting appearance of a killer storm at sea but turned out to be a stomach in need of antacid, and finally the weather: continued cold. The pond gave a quake of mournful confirmation, and when Desmond Moran arrived at a little after six, he asked for a little very hot water instead of ice in his Scotch.

Lydia, putting cheese and crackers on the coffee table, inquired with a consciously courteous air about Candide's car. Desmond, fleetingly and privately amused, said that he had driven her to the garage to pick it up and that they hadn't been able to find any engine knock. "She seemed a bit put out at whatever you said to her. She went so far as to snap at Harry."

So he was not in Candide's confidence as far as Jones Haviland went. Lydia shot him a surprised glance, and intercepted a gaze of great attentiveness. "Harry can be very snap-at-able," she said quickly. "I didn't hear any background music when I called, so I assume you haven't got a piano."

"No, I get along with a crock of nutshells. Mrs. Chilton was the most equable of grandmothers, but she was finally driven to locking her piano."

"Oh," said Lydia. *"That's* why—" and explained Harry's fast and tumbling invasion of the drawer in the telephone table that morning. "He'd have known that I didn't know the piano was off limits and he could have pounded away like a madman. Why do you suppose he does that, anyway?"

"Probably doing a study on pain thresholds, or endurance in different age groups," said Desmond vaguely. He picked up his drink, seemed to wonder what it was doing in his hand, put it down again. "Was there a key to the Blake house, by any chance?"

He never forgets, thought Lydia with the beginnings of a purely feminine anger. He's very nice—well, more than that, really—but he's only here to see what he can find out. She said crisply, "Yes, there was a key tagged Wister. There were far too many to be in current use, and I would imagine that Mrs. Chilton had forgotten she had it. As little as I knew her, I cannot imagine her prowling through other people's houses."

Desmond emptied his glass. "Difficult, too, when the Blakes keep so much to theirs . . . You're beautiful when you're angry," he concluded blandly, and Lydia laughed against her will and went to get them fresh drinks.

Dinner was a success: chicken with mushrooms—"You've had your quota of seafood," said Desmond—creamed potatoes, salad, Danish beer. They talked on neutral subjects, and the closest Desmond came to any problem area was to remark that Harry Blackwood had a certain awful fascination. "And these—think of it—are really his peak years. Visualize him in time to come, in one of the more fashionable banks, refusing loans because the people look as though they need them."

"Oh, no. In the State Department, trudging around the edges of an Aubusson rug—"

At this point, Lydia realized the focus of Desmond's earlier attention: he had been staring at her darkened eyelashes. Instantly they felt a yard long and false, and to minimize them she did not drop her gaze at all but stared widely in return. Desmond began to look understandably puzzled. Coffee came, and in her self-consciousness Lydia started when he reached across and touched her hand lightly. "To your left," he said in an undertone. "The sire."

Lydia let seconds go by and then glanced casually to her left. Harrison Blackwood was gray-haired, beautifully barbered, quietly vigilant alone at a table commanding a wide view. His board-room gaze touched Lydia's, lingered a second, returned to the dining room's entrance. Hoping, if he had spies, to surprise Candide with Jones Haviland? But the painter must have counterspies, thought Lydia, to inform him that Blackwood had not returned to New York immediately after the funeral, as might have been expected.

"How was your dinner with the Blakes?"

It was expertly offhand, going past Lydia's guard when her attention was elsewhere. "Very pleasant. I saw a painting of Emmett's this afternoon, by the way. A landscape in oils, extremely handsome."

"Oh?" The clear gaze came up. "Did they invite you over especially for that?"

"No, I'd promised Paula's sister that I'd bring back a picture of them, and one of the house."

Desmond's glance went completely still. To Lydia, it was as though a sound-proof glass bell had descended over the table, shutting away the restaurant buzz, closing her in with his total concentration. He said, not as a question, "And you took pictures."

Under that unblinking regard—which seemed more

inward; she simply happened to be in the way—Lydia felt uncomfortable and a little defensive. "It's the usual thing to do under the circumstances. In fact, it would have been peculiar not to."

". . . Yes."

It was mechanical; he would have made the same response to an observation that it was very cold for August. Then the restaurant came back, and as though he had not just seen some private world give an astonishing lurch Desmond said carelessly, "If you want to be a hundred per cent sure that your shots came out, I know a photographer in town who can print them very fast."

And also provide him with a print, to be handed around to nameless strangers. Lydia felt at the moment that she had meddled enough in Susan's life and would have no part in delving into her sister's. Desmond doubtless had a camera of his own; let him use that. "I took three or four," she lied in his own careless tone, "so at least one is bound to come out. How was your trip?"

After a single blink, he gave her a smile like an appreciative salute. "My swans turned out to be wild geese," he said.

With windows lighted randomly upstairs as well as down and the Volvo clearly visible in the driveway, the Donahue house had a surprising air of tenancy even to Lydia, who had worked out that convincing pattern of lamps. It never entered her mind that there was in fact someone waiting patiently for her inside.

When she had used her key, Desmond stepped into the living room with her to cast an automatic eye over the tranquillity. He had been quiet and abstracted on the way home from the restaurant. He said that he wouldn't stay because there might be someone trying to reach him by phone, and Lydia was startled when he lifted the tips of her lashes with a gentle finger and then kissed her lightly before the issue could become in any way debatable. "Besides," he said, turning his head alertly, "I think you have visitors arriving."

A car door slammed, and then another. Desmond went to a side window, moved a fold of velvet cautiously, reported over his shoulder, "A man in a derby and a woman with white hair. Both small and not speedy. Do you know them?"

He glanced inquiringly at her. Lydia said, "Oh, God, Uncle Frank and Aunt Lilian. Better escape while you can."

. . . Five minutes later, while she was fixing highballs in the surprisingly chilly kitchen, a different car engine came to life at the top of the hill—disciplined, with no hint of rage—and an old gray Volkswagen moved off into the icy dark.

Chapter 12

The Graces were titular relatives, inherited, Nancy Donahue had remarked once after being kept up by them until three in the morning, like a family curse. Diminutive, puce, white-haired, looking like a cross between total abstainers and health-food addicts, they had the drinking capacity and the staying power of giants. Twice a year they left the fastnesses of East Orange for Elder's Farms, bringing with them warring aromas of cigar smoke and perfume, the kind of liquor that had to be held up to the light and admired, and fragrant Jordan almonds for the children.

Mystifyingly, they seemed to come not so much to see the Donahues as to tell each other long stories about people known only to themselves. As the hours went by, mass headaches were produced by Frank's cigars, eyes glazed, throats dried from disuse. Lydia, who tonight had no idea that she owed them the ultimate in gratitude, connected them with having her nose tweaked, and also having to stay home from the beach.

"Little Lydia," they said fondly now, drinks in hand, and wanted to know all about the wedding which they had missed because a niece of Lilian's had died. Details supplied, they fell into the familiar pattern: "That reminds me of May Littauer's wedding, Frank. The oldest Howard boy was best man—" "Not the oldest, Lilian." The cigar was richly alight. "That was Roy, and he was in the Navy at the time. *He* married Dan Childers' girl, you remember, the one everybody thought was engaged to . . ."

Lydia turned her gaze politely from face to face, said essentially non-words like "Really?" and "Oh?" whenever the Graces looked expectant, presently made them another drink, stopped listening. They're my eyelashes, she thought, trying for an indignation which would not materialize, and I can dye them albino if I like . . .

Desmond also thought briefly about Lydia's lashes—he wished she hadn't drowned the gold tips—and the surprised warmth of her mouth; he wore, unconsciously, a look of contentment that turned presently into a frown.

His book had died on him, as inexplicably as a healthy infant in a perfectly safe crib. In the light of what Lydia had told him at dinner, his trip to Boston and Wrexley seemed the work of a flustery spinster peering under the bed. And yet . . . and yet—

At a bakery which stayed open late, he made a selection almost at random, carried the box out to his car, drove to the Chilton house. It wasn't much after nine and the windows were still lit as he had hoped, even on the day of the funeral. Candide answered his knock, her look of annoyance traceable, to anyone who knew her, at being caught in a utilitarian dark blue robe not unlike the nurse's in Wrexley.

"I've brought you a cheesecake," said Desmond winningly, offering the box, "and I wondered if by any chance you might have a cup of coffee to go with it?"

"Yes, of course." Candide closed the door, and somehing that had been standing in the angle of the wall behind it fell down with a clatter. A shovel. "But I was under the impression," her eyebrows went up, "that you were dining with Lydia Peel."

"I was. I did. But she remembered that her aunt and uncle were going to call from Florida," said Desmond fluently, "so we had to miss coffee."

"Oh. I'll put it right on then. Do sit down, and excuse me," said Candide, glancing discontentedly down at herself. "Harry is such a splasher in his bath . . ."

Desmond excused her with a will. When kitchen activity had given way to the sound of a door closing, he walked to the small table that held the telephone, slid the drawer quietly open, combed the contents carefully toward him. By the time Candide came back, wearing an embroidered ivory and gold Chinese robe over narrow trousers, he had the key to the Blake house in his pocket.

"Lydia is so attractive, isn't she? So"—Candide handed him coffee and a slice of cheesecake, and appeared to search daintily—"natural."

For which read unsophisticated, thought Desmond, annoyed, if not downright simple-minded. It seemed to him a very poor reward for baby-sitting with Harry that morning. He nodded at the shovel, which he had restored to its leaning position. "Is that for whacking intruders with?"

"No, it was Mother's." Although she had been back from the cemetery for less than ten hours, Candide was crisp and disapproving. "She'd bought it especially—it's strong but lightweight, and she was actually going to carry out her scheme of going about digging, if you can imagine such a thing. Harry has developed an absolute passion for it and wanted to take it to bed with him —we had quite a little scene."

Maybe, thought Desmond fragmentarily, the long robe and now the trousers were to conceal incipient bruises on her shins. He gazed at the tip of his cigarette. "Where did your mother plan to dig?"

Candide shrugged. "Knowing how I felt about the subject, she didn't really discuss it with me. She did say something about the Blake property, but I gather that they weren't enthusiastic. Oh, and she took Harry to someplace he described as a 'hole' once, and that was another thing. Excavations could be quite dangerous to a child," she said, gazing at Desmond with severity.

He was back in his apartment by ten-thirty, having asked Candide at the door—such composure was almost frightening—if she would be all right. Slaty glance flicking to the little bottle which still stood on the mantelpiece, she assured him that she would take a sleeping pill if necessary. The telephone was ringing as he left.

He poured himself a beer to erase the unfortunate cheesecake and mediocre coffee. On a mental scales he balanced his own strong instinct against Lydia's camera, and instinct came down the more heavily. He wrote for a few minutes on the back of an envelope, crossing out phrases and inserting new ones, and presently dialed a number in Manhattan.

It was Hazel Craig who answered the telephone in the apartment below his, which was just as well; her husband, although likable, was apt to be a little blurry around the edges at this time of night. Desmond answered inquiries about his health, learned that a tenant had been mugged in the lobby the week before, and put his request. "Sure," said Hazel, showing neither curiosity nor surprise—she had worked for years at the Forty-second Street Library desk—and read back to him what he had dictated.

"A Mr. Duffy called looking for you a little while ago," she said when she had finished. "He couldn't reach you up there the last couple of nights and thought you might have come back to town. He had to go off somewhere himself, but he said to tell you—*Tom!*" she shouted electrifyingly.

There was a heavy background sound, as of a piece of furniture being collided with. Something broke, with a leisurely effect. Hazel could be heard saying to her husband without rancor, "I told you so," before her voice came back to Desmond. "He said to tell you that the more he thinks about it, the surer he is that there wasn't any woman in New Orleans."

For a moment it seemed as though there were a conspiracy going, friendly, for his own good. ("Brooding over some female he thinks he saw three years ago isn't healthy.") Then Desmond had a clear image in his mind of Mrs. Chilton, doughty in her tweeds, and, hours later, the clamshell ash tray with its neat huddle of cigarette butts in the bottom and its sloping sides a virginal white. Not the ash tray of a woman who read while she smoked.

He thanked Hazel Craig, depressed the receiver button, made one more telephone call, and went to bed.

At ten-thirty the next morning, the sharp double rap of the knocker interrupted Paula Blake on the exercise mat in the room that also held her desk and typewriter. Legs suspended in bicycling position, she waited to see if Emmett would answer the door or the caller go away. At a second and more impatient knock she rolled athletically upright, poked her glasses on, threw a short striped robe over her leotard and, at the door, received a telegram addressed to Emmett.

He was in the kitchen making himself a cup of coffee, and they read it together. "Shocked and saddened to learn of Simon's death on return from Europe. Arriving Sands Hotel, Norwalk, March 14. Due to infirmity, would appreciate if you and Mrs. Blake would be my guests at lunch there 1 P.M. if convenient, so I can turn over important letter in my keeping. Welles Roland."

Today was the fourteenth. "Funny he didn't leave the letter with the lawyer," said Paula sharply.

"Maybe—"

They gazed at each other. Unlisted safe-deposit boxes were in both their minds, and then something of even greater interest. "I'll go," said Emmett, and collected his coat and drove off into the mist. He came back looking exhilarated. "Roland not only has a reservation there, he's taken a suite—apparently he has to have a chauffeur to drive him. They expect him at around noon, and there's a definite suggestion of red carpets and bowls of fruit. You'd better start getting out of that P.E. outfit."

He gave Paula a brisk spank. "Something tells me the old boy would appreciate black . . ."

From the top of the wooded hill that rose to the east of the Chilton property, Desmond watched the Blakes' departure at twelve twenty-five. The house cut off his view until a third of the way up the drive, but his field glasses were good ones and showed him two occupants in the Austin. Although he had only an hour's grace, he watched for three long minutes before he moved out from the hickory trees.

He had waked early, drunk too much coffee, paged through his dead manuscript, thought he detected a faint pulse but was too tense to do anything about it. A brand-new worry had driven him up the hill long before the Blakes could be expected to leave: had they had the locks changed when they took possession of the house?

Apart from the fact that she was known to drop sparks prodigally on her clothing, the strongest argument for Mrs. Chilton's accidental death, indeed the clinching argument, was the lack of any indication of forced entry. But her possession of a key to what had been Simon Wister's house suggested a reciprocal key, a not unusual arrangement between two friends, neither of them young, living alone. For Desmond's theory to be correct, such a key had to exist. Had the Blakes come to the same conclusion, and acted on it?

They had not—because, like Lydia, they found it inconceivable that Mrs. Chilton would ever use Wister's key. When Desmond emerged from the orchard, stared briefly at the stretch of disturbed earth just inside the stone wall and rounded the house, he was able to let himself in without difficulty.

It was not the first time he had gained admittance to premises not his own, but there was always the initial feeling of having stepped into a trap, all evidence to the contrary: houses, like garments just removed, seemed to retain the bodily impression of their users. Desmond gazed speculatively up the stairway that rose directly ahead of him, then opened one of the doors that flanked the small hall.

Living room, Wedgwood blue and white, furnished in antiques except for a comfortable fireside chair which had a look of much use. A delicate oval mirror—

the one Lydia had brought from Santa Fe?—shone between two windows. Desmond headed directly for a mahogany desk against the wall that faced the driveway. He was not naive enough to expect travel folders or sheets of paper covered with practice signatures, but it was logical to believe that even the most careful people—people with enormous reason to be careful—would relax a little with the passage of time.

He was so convinced that the center drawer would be locked, like the deep one on the bottom, that it came forward with a rush. Apart from two pens, a book of stamps, a few paper clips and a handful of cards from local merchants, it held only a large checkbook, three checks to a page: "Emmett J. or Paula L. Blake, Violet Lane, Elder's Farms, Conn." and the zip code. (A nuisance, Desmond reflected, to have to keep explaining when tendering checks that there was no telephone.) On January fifteenth the checkbook showed a balance of $903.57; by two days ago, March twelfth, the balance was $809.83. So, even if a couple with no rent to pay lived very simply, income from somewhere.

The side drawer on the right wasn't locked either. Here was the residue of minor redecorating: thumbtacks, picture hangers and wire, paint company sample folders. Under them, a letter that rocked Desmond back on his heels.

Chapter 13

The paper was the slick white available in pad form, the typing uneven, the date March eleventh. It was the signature that exploded up at Desmond. The letter was addressed to both the Blakes, and went on:

"Sorry we haven't been in touch sooner but you know how it is. I've had a job of sorts at a resort ranch owned by some friends of Naomi's near Tucson, but it's an awkward setup and we're pushing off tomorrow for Denver. The climate here is all it's cracked up to be and I've never felt better in my life. Hope you're enjoying the good life. How's your work going, and Paula's book? Naomi sends her best and we both hope you'll come out and pay us a visit when we find a place. Yours, Philip."

All present and accounted for; momentarily, the stillness of the house seemed a positive thing, won by the holding-back of laughter. Desmond searched further, grimly, but the postmarked envelope had evidently been discarded because it held no valid return address.

If a postmarked envelope had ever existed.

A fast glance at his watch sent him rapidly out of the living room. Just about now, on her lunch hour, Hazel Craig would be telephoning the Sands Hotel, purporting to be Welles Roland's secretary and leaving for the

Blakes the message that Mr. Roland had been taken ill in his car en route and forced to return to New York and a hospital for observation. Chances were that the Blakes, even in the tempting vicinity of a cocktail and lunch, would turn around and come home immediately. Desmond opened the other door in the little hall.

This room, wallpapered in green and gold wreaths of an underwater dimness, had been converted for Paula Blake's use. The only remains of its front-parlor past were a braided rug faded to mere suggestions of color and a mirror set in curlicues of mahogany. There was a long low bookcase, a businesslike desk with straight chair, an electric typewriter, a mat of some kind rolled up in one corner.

The typewriter, uncovered, was empty; the ash tray beside it contained a single cigarette end. Desmond opened a drawer, wheeled a sheet of copy paper into the machine, tapped out "Dear Paula and Emmett." As he had expected, it was a different typeface than the one used in the letter signed "Philip," elite rather than pica. Well, that would be elementary, and posed no great difficulty.

He went methodically through the other drawers. For all her unbothered working conditions, Paula Blake wasn't making much headway with her book: the forty-eight pages of yellow manuscript in a manila folder were beginning to turn beige at the edges. Nor was she as crisply efficient as her voice and her challenging gaze would seem to indicate. She hadn't cleaned out her center drawer in some time, hadn't even thrown away correspondence which must have been brought from Boston.

In spite of his sharp awareness of seconds flashing by on his wrist, Desmond took the time to sketch a rough mental picture of the drawer's appearance before he lifted out one of the letters. Chaste black McGrath Gallery, Santa Fe, N.M." on cream: it was addressed to "Dear Paula" and signed "Susan."

Susan McGrath—Desmond absorbed the fact that Paula Blake's sister, the non-flyer, was Lydia's Peel's friend with the gallery and the larcenous suitor—had the habit of dating her letters only by the day of the week, but even a fast skimming provided approximate times.

The letter he held heralded the arrival of Lydia with the mirror ("I've written you about her before—you'll like her"). In the next, fished from under a torn-out newspaper recipe and a packet of treated eyeglass tissues, Susan was trying on bathing suits and going on a diet as a result: "You know how your whole life flashes before you when you stand in front of a triple mirror." Demond slid that one back and, in a third, found a description of Thanksgiving. Susan had brightened this holiday by giving a home to a stray dog which she described as looking like an escaped mustache.

All the letters covered a wide variety of topics—the weather, the progress of her diet, books she was reading and recommended to Paula, anecdotes about the gallery, references to a man who was Miles Marsh at first and then just Miles, occasional family flashbacks: "Remember Aunt Kitty feeding us repulsive combinations of food and saying 'It all goes down the same pipe'?" Desmond found one final letter, half-imprisoned in the pages of a blank spiral notebook and nudged by a small white plastic bottle which had a faint puzzling air of familiarity.

Christmas was dealt with here. Susan had loved Paula's present, unspecified. Conscious of the time he had spent here, Desmond picked up isolated phrases at a gallop, came to a closing sentence which took on the brilliance of something in an illuminated book, had not time to absorb it fully because of the sound, distant but clear, of a car engine.

He froze incredulously where he stood, watching the driveway where the low flat-topped knoll cut it off at the curve. Had the Blakes grown suspicious, telephoned the Sands Hotel en route, received the message prematurely? From the retreating engine sound it was a car turning around, but Desmond took it as an omen and shot upstairs.

What had been a guest room at the left of the tiny landing had been cleared for use as a studio. A candlewick-covered bed was now in head-cracking position under the slope of the roof, and a low chest of drawers under the north window held an assortment of brushes in a coffee mug, squeezed tubes of paint, a many-colored rag, a heavily encrusted palette. Desmond touched the palette with a cautious finger. A faint tackiness came away, and he sensed more stifled merriment.

("Simon Wister was quite proud that his cousin was an artist," Mrs. Chilton had said in one of her rare references to Emmett Blake, "even though he was afraid they might turn out to be abstract paintings.")

Desmond did not waste time on the six or seven unframed canvases stacked against a wall, facing in—Lydia Peel had seen and admired one, which proved nothing either way—and glanced only casually at the fresh canvas stretched on the wooden easel, bearing a single sweeping curve of cobalt blue. Apparently it was to be a still life; a pottery jug of answering color and a cut-into Edam cheese on a white plate had been positioned on a table. The cheese looked, and was, extremely hard.

Standing where Blake would stand, Desmond had a direct downward view of the stretch of disturbed earth along the stone wall. Mrs. Chilton's work, with the famous shovel? For a number of reasons, he thought not. With all her insouciance, he doubted that she would have exposed herself directly to the amused eyes of the Blakes, even if they had permitted her to dig under the window where Blake worked. It seemed an unlikely spot for even the most eager amateur, and in March the ground would have been hard going for a woman in her late sixties.

Then—what? A careless gesture for Lydia Peel, who might have been confided in by Mrs. Chilton in the course of that ride home, so that she should not carry any impression of strangeness back to Santa Fe?

Desmond left the studio—no ash tray among the dresser-top clutter, he had noticed—crossed the landing, pushed open the bedroom door that stood slightly ajar. And there, smiling at him a little quizzically, as though by some atrocious feat of agility she had swarmed up the sheer side of the house, was Paula Blake.

It was twelve o'clock, a reasonably virtuous hour for the resurrecting Bloody Mary she had promised herself, when Lydia made the discovery that the enclosed stairway opening into the dining room was still in use.

It had seemed a particular outrage to wake with a hangover after an evening spent in the company of two septuagenarians. True to their fashion, the Graces had stayed until after midnight, not turning a white hair as the level in the venerable bottle of Irish whiskey sank. Frank had said meaningfully at eleven, "Does your Aunt Nancy still make those wonderful grilled cheese sandwiches? Remember those sandwiches, Lilian?" and they had both drained their glasses with a business-like air and gazed at Lydia with expectation.

The cheese sandwiches had renewed their thirst. Lydia was finally driven to slipping her shoes off and wriggling her toes to call attention to this fact; she only wished that she had a necktie to loosen and a shirt to start unbuttoning. "I believe Lydia's tired," observed Lilian half an hour later, and they had finally made their farewells.

But the night had proceeded like a day begun badly. At some point Lydia was jerked out of sleep by a small sharp crash which memory traced to the Donahues' corner bedroom, separated from her by a bath. Fatalistic in her fatigue, only getting up to investigate at all because it might be something that would burn the house down, she had gone to look and found that the clock-radio on a bedside table, which she must have brushed against in one of her anxious expeditions to the wedding-present closet, had fallen to the floor. It said three-thirty when she picked it up; a closer inspection through lashes narrowed against the light told her that it was going to go right on saying three-thirty.

At nine o'clock, feeling like a walking cigar even after she had brushed her teeth, she washed her hair in the shower, swallowed two aspirins and a cup of coffee—the Graces, she was sure, had sparkled out of bed and breakfasted hugely—and surveyed the living room. She had paused on her way to bed just long enough to remove Frank's ash tray with its noisome nest of cigar butts, and although the remaining debris was chiefly a matter of glasses and plates and napkins, Lydia could only think, in her present condition, of the Augean stables.

It was not a morning for vigorous onslaughts, it was a morning for tiptoe trips to the kitchen so that her aching head would not know what her legs were doing. Using the vacuum cleaner was for the moment unthinkable. When she had cleaned the kitchen, she surprised herself by being able to face a boiled egg and a second cup of coffee, and even to achieve—now that they were safely on their way back to New Jersey—a reluctant admiration for the Graces.

In less than twenty-four hours, she would be on her own way back to New Mexico. An imminent departure usually had the effect of transporting Lydia to her destination in every sense but the bodily; this one did not. It was a little as though she were having to hand back to its owner a puzzling book, frightening in spots, whose ending she would never know. To minimize her sense of loss, even more intimately bound up in the gray morning pricked through by tiny fiery lilac leaves and the occasional raucous mew of an off-course seagull, Lydia put it to herself in daytime-serial terms:

Will Candide Blackwood gain custody of her interesting son, Harry, and find lasting happiness with Jones Haviland, society portrait painter?

Will Desmond Moran, newspaperman, discover secrets about the intriguing Paula and Emmett Blake?

Who killed Mrs. Chilton?

It sprang as dismayingly as a spider out of a little-used drawer, something she had suspected was there but hadn't wanted to tempt. This was why she had questioned Harry, rationalized the newly dug earth at the back of the Blake house, hadn't believed Desmond's bland statement last night about his wild-goose chase, dreamed her cold dreams.

Mrs. Chilton, more alive than a lot of people half her age, had been bundled off to a frightful death. She must have seen a face over hers before she died. Emmett's, bearing or lacking some identifying feature from that long-ago visit to his cousin? Paula's, calm and matter-of-fact, like someone dealing with an animal for whom there was no other course? Jones Haviland's, bearded, bright-eyed, regretful ("Too bad, I rather liked her")? Or even, "Lie back, Mother. Lie back . . ."

This was a thought to be physically dislodged, as though the spider had begun a mincing, microscopically hairy walk inside the collar of her dress. Lydia shot to her feet, not minding the answering jar in her head, got out the vacuum cleaner, did the living-room rug and then the older, thinner Chinese Oriental in the dining room, its cream and blue less vivid but more tranquil. She put the vacuum away, feeling as always as if she had successfully penned up a berserk animal, and was dusting the top of the bookcase that held the telephone when her hip bumped the latch of the enclosed stairway and the door swung gently open.

The black iron latches in the house were responsible for countless bruises, torn pockets and oaths. The stairway, on the other hand, had been a prized escape route for Lydia and her cousins when there were unwelcome callers. On one dramatic summer night Elizabeth had fallen down it, pursued from her bedroom over the kitchen by a bat.

Lydia glanced automatically in at the curving pie-wedge steps at the bottom, and someone else had fallen prey to the inside latch quite recently: a curl of cream-colored sash, fresh and dustless, lay on the floor. It had been hooked away from a woman's robe or dress, probably in one of the gatherings before the wedding, because filtering light from a small window caught on a pair of abandoned cocktail glasses at the top of the stairs. Someone being shown this part of the house, or an amorously inclined couple slipping away from the crush.

A *good* person, said Lydia to herself, would go up and get those glasses and bring them down and wash them. Too bad there wasn't a good person around. She draped the sash over the latch on the dining-room side, because although it was nondescript enough, someone was probably wondering where it had gone, and closed the door on the down-breathing cold, which . . .

No. With the marriage and gradual departure of Tracey's older sisters, this part of the upstairs had been closed off as far as heat went, but that curious cold in the kitchen the night before had been sucked to the back when the Graces, who saved their strength for other purposes, made their leisurely progress over the threshold. Still, Lydia put the ice tray down with suddenness and went up to the Donahues' bedroom.

The closet would have been well worth raiding, with its silver and crystal and linen (including her own gift of silver-latticed liqueur glasses from Mexico), its host of glossy small appliances. But, as she had thought in her small-hours bemusement and was now able to verify, the lock on the closet door was unflawed.

She could not actually remember colliding with anything in the room, but then she constantly acquired minor cuts and bruises without realizing it at the time. In any case, even granted a would-be burglar who had read the account of the wedding and kept an eye on the house, it was inconceivable that he should have penetrated it somehow, prowled up the stairs, searched out the locked closet door, bumped against the bedside clock-radio in his haste, and simply left again.

Lydia did not look at the other side of this coin: her instant reaction if the closet door had shown a successful invasion of the house. The shocking realization that Mrs. Chilton's death had been a particularly cruel form of murder occupied a compartment of its own, unrelated to someone who in a matter of hours would start the preliminary packing for the return to Santa Fe. In picking up the cream-colored sash she had not tested it for strength between her hands. Nothing suggested the groundwork for a plan which had had to be aborted; no warning stirred in her mind at all.

Chapter 14

The realization of what he was actually looking at reached Desmond's brain fractionally too late to prevent the thunderclap response of his blood. He had been rooted in the doorway; now, like a man who had just been presented with an expertly detailed rubber snake, he moved forward for a closer look.

In the supermarket where he had turned at the overheard remark about Mrs. Chilton, Paula Blake's face had clicked into his memory as exactly as a photograph being slipped into a frame—and that was what it had been all along. No wonder he had had no recollection of any introduction. No wonder Fidge Duffy hadn't been able to recall a woman with Nicholson that night in New Orleans; he had been sitting in a different part of the hotel bedroom.

Granted the general haziness of the evening, it wasn't such a ludicrous misapprehension to have labored under. The photograph—from the spontaneity of the pose and something about the smile, Desmond suspected an enlarged close-up taken by a lucky or gifted amateur rather than a studio portrait—was the most lifelike he had ever seen. It wasn't the following-eyes effect present in certain paintings, but a quality of such immanence that it seemed possible for the glass to become misted from the inside at any moment. An accident of light and film and printing technique, Desmond reminded himself, but the initial shock was slow to die away.

If there had been an inscription, what would it have said?

He glanced across the room at a bureau obviously used by Paula Blake, but there was no answering photograph of her husband. Come to that, Desmond hadn't seen a single other photograph in the house. It was true that there were people—he was one of them—who considered festooning family faces on mantels and tabletops to be an invasion of everybody's privacy, but he would have expected to find a snapshot of Paula's Santa Fe sister somewhere, and certainly one of a younger Emmett Blake whom Simon Wister planned to make his heir. Unless Blake, out of modesty . . . ? Desmond gave that a little thought and discarded it out of hand.

A random glance in at the top bureau drawer revealed that Blake was such a tidy fellow that a handkerchief out of line at the bottom of a neatly folded pile was noticeable. It wasn't a handkerchief. It was the edge of one of four snapshots of Paula Blake, taken, like the framed photograph, without her glasses. Desmond puzzled over that, remembered that in the supermarket she had been swinging her glasses in her hand, examined the snapshots.

There were variations of pose, but the background was the same in all four: the front door of the house, showing the brass knocker in the form of a simple ring. She stood in full sunlight, and although "February" was printed on the margins, she wasn't clad for what Desmond vividly remembered of February; she wore only slacks and a loose cream pullover. She must have gotten cold indeed, posing outside with the temperature in the low twenties.

And suddenly, without doubt, without even glancing at his watch, Desmond knew that it was time to get out of there, at speed. He pocketed one of the snapshots, slid the others back under the handkerchiefs. At the foot of the stairs he made sure that he was taking away with him the crumpled sheet with the comparison typing on it, reset the lock, stepped outside, closed and tested the front door. His back prickled all the while, as if someone behind him held a dart in throwing position.

He had left his field glasses among the hickory trees at the top of the hill. Breathing hard, his mended shoulder and collarbone sending out an aching complaint, he bent, straightened, turned for another scan of the property below him. The glasses traveled over that peculiarly glib stretch of dug ground, the knoll which hid the driveway's curve. At the gentle crest, long coarse grass leaped at him, surprisingly sharp and clear, with a longish edge of shadow behind it.

It wasn't a fold in the ground. He was looking at an excavation of some kind—not a trash pit, which would hardly be situated on a rise in any case, but something of regular proportions.

The knoll was a natural site for a house, or, going farther back in time, a cabin.

Was this Harry's "hole"? Candide had spoken of it as though it were divorced from the Blake property. In view of her expressed impatience and displeasure, Desmond could imagine Mrs. Chilton being blandly content to let her think so.

He snapped the glasses down from his eyes, because the hood of the Austin rounding the curve seemed about to smash into his face. He had stepped automatically back into the trees; now, remembering something Candide had said the evening before, he started urgently down the other side of the hill toward the studio.

"I suppose that could be called fun of a sort, if you like driving to Norwalk and back for nothing," said Paula Blake sourly as they entered the house. "Make us a drink while I get out of this dress, will you? You needn't keep too sharp an eye on the jigger."

The dress wasn't black, but the demurest thing she owned: gray wool with a deep crisp ruffle of white that cupped her throat like a tulip. It would have soothed the eye of an infirm old family friend, had one existed. Paula started for the stairs, putting a hand up and back to the zipper-pull, changed her mind, with great gentleness eased the door of her workroom open just wide enough to slip through. After a single glance she called sharply, "Emmett!"

When they had first moved into the house, it had seemed wise to be able to know if anyone had entered it during their absence, although they almost never left it together: "After all, we have to be on the alert for art thieves," said Paula to Emmett. Out of the toe of a nylon, stuffed with the rest of the stocking, she had contrived a weightless little ball to place in near-invisibility on the wide honey-colored floorboards just inside the door before she closed it.

Now they gazed together at the nylon ball, which lay an inch or two in on the rug at the natural end of an arc. Emmett asked after a small pause, "Are you *sure* you . . ." and Paula said, "Absolutely. You can't tell how long lunches will last, and something told me it would be a good idea."

They contemplated each other in the kind of communicating silence which made so many of their utterances elliptical. "I think," said Emmett, "that we'd better have a very good look around."

Why had Philip Nicholson possessed, and traveled with, a photograph of his friend's wife? Try something harder, Desmond advised himself, like the one about the chicken crossing the road.

Equally, looking back, he suspected that Paula Blake knew nothing about that particular fact. She had been completely unshaken by his query in the library because she had never been in New Orleans and was unaware of the peripatetic photograph. Emmett Blake, beside her, hadn't turned a hair either, hadn't shown the slightest interest in a surprising question put by a total stranger.

Blake . . . ?

The nurse in Newton had told him that Philip Nicholson would have lost a good deal of weight in his bout with pneumonia and then an adverse reaction to antibiotics. The fair-haired Blake was on the lean side for his height, and although Desmond hadn't felt a flicker of recognition on being introduced, his actual memory of Nicholson was vague, his concentration on Paula Blake so sharp that it was like a knife that had lost its edge for the next job.

One thing stood clearly out of the whole roiling mess: the last sentence in Susan McGrath's post-Christmas letter to her sister. "I don't know about you, but I've found the dividend checks an absolute godsend this year."

Just *the* dividend checks, requiring no explanation between them. The inescapable conclusion was that

Paula Blake received dividend checks too—from a trust of some kind, established for children who might still materialize? Whatever the source, the incoming cash would explain the scarcely depleted checking account.

There was another aspect to be looked into, literally, as soon as possible. Desmond dialed Candide's number, thinking that it would be just as well if she hadn't seen him coming down the hill, and said to her obviously disappointed voice, "If you're still planning to leave later today, is there anything I can do for you in the way of errands? Maybe—you must have your hands full—I could take Harry out for a drive or something?"

"Actually, that would be very kind," said Candide after a few seconds of understandable astonishment. "Just a minute, and I'll ask him." The phone went down, and Desmond heard patches: "Mr. Moran . . . Darling, you know he doesn't have a cat, we were there yesterday . . . Well, Mummy wants you to. He'd like that very much," she said firmly to Desmond. Then, faintly and automatically arch, "Did you have any luck with your bird watching? That *was* you, wasn't it, on the hill?"

"Yes. I saw a very fine nuthatch," said Desmond. "Suppose I come over right away?"

Because he could not hope that the Blakes would leave the house again today, after a frustrating car trip which must have left them irritable even if not suspicious, but now they ought to be occupied with lunch. What with Candide's departure to the undoubtedly spurious, sheltering friends in Boston, he might not have another chance with Harry. Who, young though he was, should be able to recognize his "hole" without difficulty.

As in a child's game of dots which made a pattern,

Desmond drew a mental line from the shovel to the excavation to Mrs. Chilton's death by fire only hours after her visit to the Blakes. He did not go beyond that for fear of etching a picture in the very atmosphere.

Children did not as a rule care for any hint of manipulation, and Harry Blackwood differed only in the extent of dislike. His flowerlike face was set like concrete, his greeting to Desmond a measured "You need to wash your hands."

"Darling, that's not very nice," said Candide without heat, but Desmond, glancing at a small spot of cobalt blue from Emmett Blake's palette on his right index finger, felt a profound gratitude. "He's right," he said, and then, because Candide's gaze had turned attentive, "Touch-up paint for the car—somebody clipped my door in a parking lot."

Harry, as cooperative as a department-store dummy, was allowing his arms to be maneuvered through the sleeves of his coat. Candide, busying herself with the buttons, said with a lift of her eyebrows, "You're very punctilious over a rental car," and Desmond said simply and unanswerably, "I try harder."

Two minutes later he was out in the car with Harry. Two minutes and fifteen seconds later, Harry had discovered that by half-lying on the seat and pushing with his extended leg, he could make the lid of the glove compartment come clattering down, snap it shut again, and repeat the process. Desmond bore this in silence, as it was imperative to stay on the right side of Harry until his mission had been accomplished, but he wondered what private plans he had interrupted. Harry's forte was the scrutinizing, hair-counting stare, or geometric trudging.

"Are we going to see Daddy?" inquired Harry mufflledly into his coat collar.

Desmond gave him a startled sidelong glance. In their short acquaintance Harry had appeared to find it quite natural that his father had disappeared from his life, but young children of divorce must, by the very pressure of events, build a protective shell. "Well, no," he said. "Would you have liked to?"

"No," said Harry unequivocally.

So much for that. Desmond let a silence go by before he remarked, "I think I've found a good place to dig, when you get your shovel."

Harry sat upright. "Mummy said no," he said, and folded his arms militantly.

And Candide was not going to be pleased if and when Harry told her about this expedition—but Desmond was sorry for her trouble, because what had been a hypothesis was hardening into a conviction. Mrs. Chilton's enthusiasms had been total while they lasted, and along with her courtesy went an inflexible stubbornness. If the Blakes' coldness toward her was a determination not to let her dig in whatever that excavation was, she might—with the feeling that her long friendship with Simon Wister gave her implicit privilege—have been spurred on. She would certainly not have dropped her project meekly.

Desmond's skin prickled, but then his head also ached—a gift from the flu-stricken nurse in Wrexley? He said to Harry, "It wouldn't hurt to take a look," and swung the car in on the verge opposite the Blakes' lilac-hidden driveway.

Here he came face to face with an unforeseen obstacle; Harry did not want to get out of the car. Having gathered by osmosis that this place was of particular interest to Desmond, he pulled up his knees and hunched his shoulders and said piteously that he was cold and he didn't feel well. Where didn't he feel well? All over. Desmond, in whom this response from nieces and nephews not wanting in emergencies to go to doctors or dentists struck a chord, opened the door and said, "Harry. Out."

Harry studied him and then climbed out of the car with dignity. Inside the driveway, they went past an asparagus bed where thick purplish heads were beginning to emerge, and then up the side of the knoll. From here, only the upper windows of the house were visible —and this sunken rectangular space, when Desmond had walked a few more steps, was unmistakably an old foundation. Half-burned boards were overlaid by dead branches, crumbled bricks, a multitude of other small debris, all of it looking fairly recent. When they weren't typing or painting, the Blakes were cleaning up their property.

Had Mrs. Chilton seen it like that when she first acquired her shovel? And what had she hoped to find by probing away at the earth—old glass? Arrowheads? Certainly she would not have brought Harry there with any other surmise. He said very casually, "Well, what do you think of it?" and Harry said scornfully, "It's just an old hole. Grandmama told me."

To throw her daughter off the scent? Desmond, who supposed that he should have despised himself for catechizing a child under the circumstances but did not, said, "Was all this stuff in here when you and your grand—" and stopped dead.

The Austin was quiet, and it had appeared around the curve below them without warning. The hand brake sounded audibly, and Paula Blake emerged and started up the knoll. Sun striking off her glasses, she said crisply, "This is private property, so if you'd please—oh. I've met you, haven't I?"

"Desmond Moran—yes, in the library, Mrs. Blake. How are you?" His heart had picked up a sharp beat. "This is Harry Blackwood, who"—he strolled closer and looked conspiratorial—"thinks he dropped a silver dollar Mr. Wister once gave him in here. He's leaving town with his mother later on today, so I told him we'd give it a try even though—"

"I did not!" said Harry, behind him.

Bless his little pebble of a heart. Desmond glanced elaborately at the sky, a man in search of patience. "A reaction to yesterday, I imagine," he told Paula Blake in a still lower and even more confidential tone. "You know. Sublimating the whole business, fabricating trifles. Natural enough, but trying on a parent in the throes of removal, so I volunteered."

Harry knew very well when he was being talked above. He yanked at Desmond's sleeve and shouted angrily, "I did not what you said!"

I'll kill him at my leisure, thought Desmond, and said, "Now, Harry," in a gently reproving voice. He lifted his glance to Paula Blake. "I'm sorry, I would have phoned to ask permission if I'd been able."

Paula Blake did not say "That's perfectly all right" or any other social, throw-away thing. She dropped her green gaze to Harry coolly. "I'm afraid you couldn't find your dollar even if it is in there, we've done so much burning."

Harry's dancing rage now looked capable of driving him to tears, and Desmond could not take his paint-stained right hand out of his pocket for anchoring purposes. From the direction of the house, a clear whistle began. As though it had been a steam kettle, Paula Blake called instantly, "Emmett!" and ran a few steps away. "Check the oven, will you? I think I left it on."

Desmond took this opportunity to seize Harry's hand with his own left one, and said good-bye and apologized lightly for trespassing. Again, Paula Blake did not tell him that it was of no concern. She said, "Sorry, Harry," which nearly started him off again, and gave them both a fleeting smile and, in her car, occupied herself with lighting a cigarette and inspecting her makeup in the mirror so that they were out of the driveway before she started the engine. Desmond, starting his own, lifted a hand as he drove away.

Harry refused to speak to him all the way back to the house, but Harry's participation was no longer strictly necessary. Desmond had found the "hole," burned over several times, probably added to in the way of fill. If Mrs. Chilton were still alive with her shovel, and her determination, she would have had to do exactly what he was going to have to do.

Dig a little deeper.

Chapter 15

Lydia had the Volvo's tank filled and the battery, oil and tires checked—preparations, it seemed to her, almost as final as snapping the locks on a suitcase. She had fallen into a foreign-car conversation with the attendant, who looked about fourteen but turned out to be the owner of a Mercedes-Benz, and it was after two o'clock when she got back to the house.

The all-day silence of the telephone did not suggest any kind of quiet and concentrated meshing, even when Candide finally called. "Lydia." It was clear from her tone that she did not have any farewell thank-you's in mind. "I've been trying to reach you for nearly an hour. How much did you tell Desmond Moran about Jones?"

Lydia was so astonished at this inquisitional displeasure that it took her a moment to remember the painter. "Not a thing," she said shortly. "The subject did not arise."

"Well, it's *most* odd then." Candide's voice stopped barely short of disbelief. "Desmond came by a little while ago, to take Harry for a drive, he said—I told him when he dropped in for coffee last night that I'd be busy today closing up the house—which seemed a little strange as I must say he isn't terribly good with children. *And* he had paint on his hand. He had some ridiculous story about touching up his car, but he's obviously been prowling around Jones's studio."

Lydia had to remind herself that to Candide the world was a series of concentric circles of which she occupied the heart. "Why on earth would he do that? Why would he care about you and Jones?"

There was a chilly, bridling silence, as if she had asked why the sun came up. Then, "*I* don't know, but he is a newspaperman," said Candide, "and I've just called the inn and Harrison is still registered there."

Lydia, whose attention had gone off in an entirely different direction, nevertheless managed to put forward a number of non-worrying explanations: Harrison might have discovered some tempting real estate in the town, fallen wildly in love with one of the maids, broken his leg. Surprisingly, Candide received these with civility. "You're probably right and it's nothing to do with me at all. Still, I did want to check with you . . ."

It wasn't Jones Haviland's studio Desmond had been prowling around, thought Lydia, hanging up presently. It was Emmett Blake's, to which, last night, she had as good as handed him entry. He had gone to Candide's for the purpose of wangling the key, and he had proceeded from the Blakes' to collect Harry—Harry, who coveted his grandmother's shovel.

Again, she had a feeling of having set something irretrievably in motion. If she had never appeared on the scene with the mirror, never mentioned the Blakes in Desmond's hearing . . . You're getting like Candide, said Lydia to herself, and went to the beach.

* * *

Desmond had said with his air of casual intimacy that he would see her today, so after some hesitation she left a note on the door. As looking for Scotch tape in other people's houses was a fruitless as looking for shoestring potatoes in strange supermarkets, she attached the note with a common pin she found in an ash tray on the piano. White on white, it was invisible from the road and would not be a statement of non-occupancy.

The beach was in a large sense the summation of Lydia's childhood, and she did not want to carry away with her the brooding hostility she had met on her first visit. It would be low tide, but with the sun finally out she could photograph the long arm of rocks that enclosed this crescent of Sound, the archaic bathhouse, the nostalgic floats.

There were no dog-exercising driftwood gatherers here today; she had the beach to herself. Lydia parked the car near the bathhouse and walked down a long raised finger of planking that disappeared into the water at high tide but was now redolent, from underneath, of exposed sand, barnacled rocks, rotting seaweed, defunct-smelling creatures which had not made it back with the tide. A few seagulls rose noisily at her approach, descended again, regrouped in their busy strutting search.

Lydia used up the rest of her film, turned with the camera, lifted her head sharply. A seagull, or other bird or cat, was trapped in the bathhouse; even over the wind she could hear a distressed and mewing cry. She went back up the boardwalk, and the sound was louder. She thought suddenly and horrifyingly of a newborn infant: people who abandoned them in garbage cans would scarcely jib at the bathhouse. Lydia was not enthusiastic about investigating, but she could not carry that reproachful echo about with her for the rest of her days. She stepped into the first of four doorless entrances and, surrounded by the pungency of damp wood, old bathing suits, pervading salt, was ten years back in time.

To her left was the life guard's office, where out-of-town people had to pay for beach stickers and minor injuries were attended to; it was so shadowy now that it was hard to believe it would come to life in June. To her right, the first long narrow aisle with changing-rooms opening off it was bisected by shorter laterals. From perhaps seven feet below, light glimmered occasionally up between the rough boards; the rest was near-darkness. Lydia walked a few steps down the aisle. "Cat?" she said, feeling foolish, and was answered by an identifiable meow from several feet away.

"Stupid animal," said Lydia to bolster herself, because all at once, in spite of her relief that it was not a baby, she was acutely nervous. A young boy had hanged himself here one summer, choosing one of the cubicles with a hook still remaining on the door, and after that the locks had been removed. Where the wind could penetrate, and in this dilapidated building that was almost everywhere, the doors moved gently on more darkness. There was something eager about the stirring, as though her hollow footsteps had been awaited for a long time.

Cat, said Lydia, but this time silently, you are going to have to get out of here the best way you can. She was not nervous now, she was sharply frightened. Once, the summer after the hanging, she had been walking along one of these aisles in perfect nonchalance when a sudden sense of mortal danger sent her sprinting toward the daylight, collecting a murderous splinter along the way, as though she had left her escape almost too late.

A meow was the simplest of sounds to imitate. It didn't require a cat at all.

This reflection, plus the recaptured warning: *Run!* saved her. She had already pivoted and was in motion when there was a shocking eruption of human presence behind her and an arm started to clip itself about her throat.

Lydia wrenched herself sideways and free, hit the rough plank wall with staggering force, did not dare look over her shoulder and risk her balance again, began to run. Light indicating the second entrance—and a sawhorse blocking it, the planks had given way. She was incapable of screaming and did not even realize that she was making an indefinable sound full of built-in despair: from its muscled strength the arm belonged to a man, and he was almost close enough to seize her around the neck again.

She would never make the third entrance. Left, then, and into a possible dead end where the softly pounding feet could corner her at their leisure? It was still the only chance. Lydia hurled herself wildly left, saw sunlight and the pavilion at the end of the corridor, knew that she would come out twenty feet short of the wooden steps down, jumped instead.

The bathhouse sloped here, and it was a jarring but not a crippling fall. Lydia picked herself up and began to run blindly for the car at the far end; it had not penetrated her consciousness that there had been no following impact. She reached the Volvo, got the door open—she had left it unlocked in this windswept vacancy—pushed the lock buttons down, stared tremblingly through the windshield.

She couldn't drive, shaking like this.

She had to drive.

She managed the key into the ignition, tried for first gear, got reverse instead, stalled the engine. It was not the time to cry. She was safe in the car even if he came exploding out of the bathhouse, but her nerves did not accept that. Lydia started the engine again, took a number of long deep breaths, found first gear, moved jerkily forward in a bucking fashion she hadn't achieved since her driving test.

And she wasn't as alone as she had thought, although the gray Volkswagen parked near the yacht basin indicated a boatowner busy about caulking or scraping or painting, too far away to hear even if she had screamed.

Lydia did not stop until she was well clear of the beach. She smoked a steadying cigarette, absorbing the sounds and sights of safety—perfectly normal traffic, the campaign poster of a woman running for the town council, which someone had decorated with glasses and a beard. She thought of calling the police from the first public telephone booth she saw—what if a child followed that mewing into the bathhouse?—but when she found one there was no parking within a block, and her legs weren't equal to the walk even if she could approximate the curb. Lydia, glancing automatically down, saw with detached surprise that although she had no sensation of pain and could not remember hurting herself, her left knee was deeply scraped and bloodied; the stain had seeped through her skirt-edge.

She had paused at a light, keeping the car tensely in first so that she would not find the wrong gear and ram the driver behind her, when the unmistakable signal of a horn showed her Desmond Moran, bound the other way. She indicated that she was going home, and in her rear-view mirror saw him pause and make an illegal U-turn to follow her.

. . . And she was in the driveway, alive, safe. When she had switched off the engine, she simply sat there trying for control of the muscles which, having done her bidding to get her here, now seemed to be engaged in a kind of loose dance. She got out of the car when Desmond emerged from his, said containedly, "I was—there was a man at the . . ." and broke helplessly into tears.

Desmond held out his arms, and one of them moved forward. Lydia said against his shoulder, inside his gentle hold, "I didn't think I'd get away, Desmond. I really didn't think I would get—"

He took her house key from her. He knew where the bathroom was and after a look at her knee he started the water running. He also knew where the liquor was and poured her a brandy before he asked any questions at all. Somehow, reduced in essence to "I thought I heard a cat or maybe a baby crying, and someone jumped out at me instead," it did not sound so very terrible. It might almost have had a prankish ring: the retaliation of teen-age boys against an adult who had intruded on some private rite. (But even then there was a point where, like laughter become hysteria, mock-savagery turned into the real thing.)

In any case there had been nothing prankish about that arm leaping out of darkness. There had been a focused intent to harm, and only the recollection of an old terror had deflected it. Lydia was sure that if she had been startled into immobility for so much as the blink of an eyelash she would not be here now, she would be behind one of those doors, permanently unaware of light or darkness or a stirring which would not be anticipatory any longer, but lazy and appeased.

She gave a quick involuntary shiver, and Desmond, who had started to ask, "Was the Volkswagen—" changed his mind and said, "You'd better get that knee cleaned up and I'll call the police. There certainly won't be anyone there now, but they ought to know and it might make them keep an eye on the place occasionally."

Lydia added fresh hot water to the bath, which felt infinitely safe and comforting once she had gotten past the wincing business of cleaning the ground-in sand and dirt out of her knee. The tip of her shoulder, where she had caromed off the bathhouse wall, had begun a dull premonitory aching. By concentrating, she could catch the end of Desmond's conversation with the police:

"No, she wasn't . . . No, she didn't." Pause. "Because, I assume, it was dark and she is not a six-foot male and simply wanted to get the hell out of there . . . Right. Thanks."

The receiver went down, accompanied by a muttered imprecation, then Desmond said immediately outside the bathroom door, "Are you alive and well in there?"

Lydia said that she was.

"You have soap."

"Yes."

"And a towel, I suppose."

"Two," said Lydia, smiling at the ceiling; she knew why he was doing this, and appreciated it.

"In short, everything you need. Well, if there's nothing I can get you," said Desmond, "I'll go out and see if I can find out what happened to your note."

It had been gone from the door when he stopped by,

but a common pin was not the most secure means of attachment. Lydia got presently out of her bath, searched for and finally found a gauze square for her still-oozing knee. When she had put on her long robe, she gave her face and hair a little attention—she must have looked like a madwoman—and still had time to smoke most of a cigarette before Desmond came back in with the note—"3:15. Gone to the beach"—which it was hard to believe she had written not much more than an hour ago. "Must have been quite a wind," he said. "It was at the end of the grape arbor."

The latticed arbor, now wearing a scrawny beard of dead-looking Concord vines, was to the rear and side of the house. There were never enough grapes for making jelly, and they weren't satisfactory for eating purposes, but it had been one of the ceremonies of summer for Lydia and her cousins to watch for the clusters to assume their deep frosty bloom and then sit in the dappled light inside the arbor, sucking the sweet skins and spitting out the tart pulp.

But in March no one would be keeping an eye on the arbor. If she had been—incapacitated in the bathhouse, thought Lydia, how long before Desmond, the only person to miss her as she had in effect said good-bye to the others, would have thought of looking at the beach? It was true that she had mentioned going there to Candide, in answer to an insincere invitation to drop in for a cup of tea, and the Blakes knew of her earlier visit because she had told them about the driftwood. But by the time her absence had become a matter of concern, Candide would probably have left Elder's Farms and it would not have occurred to Desmond—at once, anyway—to ask questions of people he distrusted. The tide would have come swelling darkly back in, paused, commenced its tireless, pebble-pulling ebb . . .

"You started to ask me something about the Volkswagen," said Lydia hastily, and Desmond said yes; had it been there when she arrived at the beach?

Gulls, wind, an impression of vacancy although she hadn't consciously been looking for other cars . . . "I don't think so," said Lydia, "but then gray Volkswagens sort of fade into the landscape."

"They do indeed," agreed Desmond with a touch of grimness. Then, before Lydia could wonder about that, "Did you manage to hang onto your camera in all this?"

With the instinctive reaction of the fingers to retain possession of whatever they were holding at the time of a fall, she had—and, thought Lydia, Full circle. Back to the camera. She had imagined the relationship between them to be changed since she had headed into his open arms, but it was simply a case of "Step into my parlor." This man was single-minded, and she had been fool enough to forget that.

"Yes, I did. It's in the car. And did you," inquired Lydia in a light stung voice, "manage to leave the Blakes' house tidy behind you?"

Chapter 16

The sharp silence that followed was, for Lydia, like the flinching wait for the impact of some dropped and highly breakable object. Desmond studied her, eyebrows up. He said musingly, "Now who told you about that, I wonder?"

"Nobody." In some unfair way he had managed to transfer any defensiveness to Lydia. It might have been his steady regard, which had a measuring element. "But you obviously suspect the Blakes of something, and you asked about a key to their house last night, and you have paint on your—"

She stopped short, forced to follow Desmond's mild inspection of his perfectly clean hands, engulfed in heat from head to toe.

"Look before you leap. I took it off," explained Desmond kindly. He seemed to be contemplating her color with interest, and Lydia felt it deepen. "You've been talking to Candide, I take it—I thought she took quite an interest at the time. Odd. I was under the impression that she hadn't met either one of the Blakes until the night of the fire."

He was inviting her to be sidetracked; Lydia refused. She said steadily, "And did you find whatever you were looking for, at the Blakes'?"

"I think so," said Desmond after a fractional hesitation. "I think the Blakes are blameless."

It struck Lydia as a strange, hair-splitting choice of words; it was even stranger that neither of them had mentioned Mrs. Chilton or murder. Or perhaps it wasn't. From the beginning, where the Blakes were concerned, they had been like two people wary of changing seats in a canoe; that was the existence of Susan, to whom she felt responsible. She said lightly, "You don't seem particularly happy about it."

Desmond gave an easy shrug. "People who like being wrong are generally locked up somewhere." He had finished his cigarette and he put it out briskly with an air of disposing of the whole subject at the same time. "I mentioned your camera a while ago because if you took several pictures at the beach, you might just have something on film that you didn't notice at the time."

If there had been the slightest indication of anyone lurking in the bathhouse, Lydia would not have entered for any reason at all, but she supposed that, technically, he had a point. Enlarged photographs had been known to turn up surprising detail—and she was suddenly tired of fighting on this front, particularly as Desmond had had the freedom of the Blake house a short time ago. A photograph of them, easily obtainable on his own with a little patience, now seemed minor. She said, "I doubt it very much, but you're welcome to take the film to your photographer friend if you like."

"I will. You never know," said Desmond, coming to his feet. The fact that he did so without apparent haste seemed to Lydia a measure of control rather than any lack of urgency. At the door he gave her a searching look, hesitated with his hand on the knob, made up his mind, said, "I shouldn't be long, but lock this, will you? And don't be alarmed if you see a boy outside—he's a young friend of the Donahues' who does yard work when the spirit moves him." He had the front door open; he added, "Don't go anywhere," and departed.

As Lydia was robed, aching, inclined to limp and beginning to feel the first tremors of reaction, the last injunction might have been faintly funny except for the one before it. Cause for alarm at seeing a stranger outside could only lie in the premise that the man in the bathhouse had undoubtedly seen the blue Volvo, might know where it belonged—Lydia hadn't encountered another one like it in the town—and come after her because he was wanted for previous and successful attacks and couldn't be entirely sure that she had no way of identifying him.

But that was little short of ridiculous, she thought, alone in the house which seemed suddenly to have enlarged itself and sprouted more doorways, when he hadn't bothered to pursue her in her jump to the sand. Although she probably owed that to the presence of the gray Volkswagen . . .

And was that darkish flicker outside the arrival of the yard boy? No; a wind had come up, stirring trees and bushes about in the graying afternoon like a spoon in a giant pitcher. Lydia had already locked the front door and was sure of the back. It would do no harm, she told herself with as much nonchalance as if she were reassuring someone else, to inspect the windows.

The film Desmond had taken from the camera in the Volvo rested in his pocket like a long-awaited report from a doctor, but before he did anything about it, he made one stop. The Donahues did not employ a yard boy but Mrs. Chilton had, on occasion: a high school junior as tall as Desmond, whose passions were divided equally between his karate classes and his motorcycle. On the occasions when his motorcycle was being taken lovingly apart, he had sent brothers of approximately the same size—and all that was needed at the Donahue house, for the next hour or two, was a loitering and resourceful presence.

Because if he was right, Lydia must not be left alone. If he was wrong all the way, and the episode at the beach was just one more act of random violence, she must not be irretrievably alienated. She had felt as though she belonged against his shoulder after that panicky flight from her car, but her loyalties seemed absolute.

Desmond did not know the last name of his seventeen-year-old quarry—Mrs. Chilton had referred to him only as "Hatch"—but he had once given one of the brothers a lift back into town and he found the shabby, comfortable-looking yellow house without difficulty. Hatch seemed to be in sole possession, but a third element had entered his life: a small blonde girl who came proprietarially up behind him and laced her arms around his waist while Desmond was putting his request. A television screen in the background showed a pattern of flipping-over horizontal lines; in the course of watching this interesting presentation, Hatch's hair had become wildly rufled.

"Gotcha," said Hatch, when persuasive money had changed hands. He looked at the sky. "What if it starts to get dark?"

"Pretend you can't start your bike." The girl, who would be pretty when her skin cleared up, peeked intermittently around the boy's back like a hand puppet;

Desmond found himself having to concentrate on Hatch's young but reliable-looking face. "Just don't leave until I get back there. In the flesh," he added, thinking of telephoned messages, and some of his urgency got past the girl's antic behavior. Hatch freed himself briskly, said over his shoulder, "Wait here, okay?" and seconds later was kicking his motorcycle into deafening life. Desmond glanced at his watch and went in search of Will Tadlock.

Tadlock, an occasional fishing companion of Tom Donahue's, was a likable, faintly disreputable jack-of-all-trades. Among other going enterprises he took passport photographs at his house, which was equipped with a darkroom; economy-minded brides-to-be sometimes went for their portraits and emerged wanting only strings of numbers across their lacy bosoms.

There was no point in telephoning him because when he was not in his darkroom or his rowboat he was careening about in an old pick-up, dealing mysteriously in tires and sheet metal. His wife left him periodically and, when she was in residence, refused spitefully to take messages. His activities, even on the domestic side, agreed with him to such an extent that to Desmond, who had bought him a drink at the tavern a few nights earlier, he looked unchanged after a dozen years.

There were chickens squawking noisily around the almost grassless yard on the edge of town, and the only vehicle in sight among piles of bricks, coiled wire and stacked firewood was a Fiat, crumpled like an accordion with its doors hanging open. Desmond mounted the steps of the small shingled house and knocked anyway, trying mentally to track Hatch on his motorcycle. He should be at the Donahues' by now, a large and frankly interested witness to the arrival of any—

"If you're looking for my husband, he isn't home, as usual," said the woman who had snapped open the door.

Mrs. Tadlock was back, however temporarily, and although Desmond had never met her except by hearsay, it was possible at once to see the advantages of a darkroom and a rowboat. She was alarming-looking: late forties, thin as a rake, with straw-colored hair in bangs, hot brown eyes set in circles of only slightly paler brown, generous scrolls of lipstick to take up where Nature had never even begun, a voice suitable for the shattering of glass. The thick curls of cigarette smoke that surrounded her ought by rights to have been visible emanations of dangerous energy.

Desmond identified himself, and said that he had a film to be developed, of a very urgent nature. Perhaps he could leave it here—such was Mrs. Tadlock's power that he might have been proposing an obstreperous child or a vicious animal—but in the meantime did she have any idea of where he might find Will?

"Me, he asks!" shrieked Mrs. Tadlock. "I ask that man where he's going, it's my right, isn't it, and he says hither and yon. Wouldn't that grab you? Hither and yon. I can tell you when he will be back, though, he'll be back in time to shut up those stupid chickens. I told him when he got them, I said, 'I'll wring their necks and glad to when the time comes but everything else is up to you.'" She fixed Desmond with a burning eye. "Would you want to come in and wait?"

"Thanks very much, but I'm late already. Could I use your phone, though?"

"Be my guest," said Mrs. Tadlock, lighting another cigarette and stepping back. The thick little clouds of smoke were explained by the fact that she didn't inhale but simply sent out short nervous bursts like a machine gun. "If it's a local call."

Desmond assured her that it was, and located the telephone in a small living room that also contained an upright piano, a couch, two overstuffed chairs, a coffee table, a large television set, hassocks, a whatnot, and a stand holding an enormous and unattractive plant with spearlike leaves. "You wouldn't believe the cuttings I get from that," observed Mrs. Tadlock before she retired to the doorway to listen. "A dollar and a quarter I sell them for. They grow like crazy."

". . . Lydia?" Desmond's turned shoulder brought him almost nose to nose with a velvet-painted kitten peeping out of a ribboned basket, safe forever from Mrs. Tadlock's zestful drowning. "Did the yard boy get there?"

"No . . . wait a minute, yes, I see him." If Lydia was surprised at this concern for the Donahue grounds, it wasn't apparent; she had a question of her own. "Did you happen to open one of the dining-room windows while you were here?"

"No." Even a low-set and unlocked window wasn't necessarily suggestive, Desmond knew—the Donahues hadn't been leaving a fortress behind them, after all, and Lydia herself might have opened the window without thinking and forgotten to re-lock it when she closed it—but he took a tighter grip on the receiver. "If you're nervous at all, ask Hatch to come in. He's a nice kid."

As he hung up, something puzzling was driven from his mind by what sounded like physical combat breaking out in the kitchen. This proved to be Mrs. Tadlock slamming cupboard doors and whacking glasses and a bottle of homemade wine onto the kitchen table, saying fiercely, "Even if you can't wait for Will, you have time for a glass of wine, raw cold afternoon like this."

From the challenging glance she gave him as she poured, she was a woman to whom hospitality was not an offer but a command, and the declining of it for any reason a calculated insult to be repaid at some future time. She had a practiced air of having forced drinks into reformed alcoholics, rich desserts into desperate dieters, spicy foods into ulcer patients. Desmond thought it quite probable that she would throw away the film and the note he had scrawled for Will if she were crossed, and he drank, standing, a glass of wine which he could imagine a connoisseur being driven to describe as "a mischievous little Drāno."

He also bought a bottle of the wine for two dollars, because Mrs. Tadlock's gaze still seemed to need quenching. As benevolent in her triumph as it was possible for her to be, she kicked a chicken off the front steps and promised to have her husband develop the film as soon as he got home. Desmond wondered why he ever came home, and drove rapidly toward the Chilton house.

Candide had greeted him with considerable chill on his return with her son that afternoon, with, under the chill, something that in another woman might have been apprehension. Both had vanished when Harry, tongue tripping over itself in his eagerness to draw down thunder and lightning on Desmond's head, had given an account of the expedition to the Blake property. He ended up with a baleful, "He told a *lie,*" but all Candide said was, mildly, "Darling, is that nice?"

Puzzling. Some worry off her shoulders, and not to do with the excavation. Would Candide, Desmond wondered now, fall in with what would be a sensible request from her point of view and give him a key to the house, just in case? Sanctuary for Lydia on this last dangerous night in Elder's Farms, with the Volvo remaining in the Donahue driveway.

He was aware that to place emphasis on a gray Volkswagen at the beach because the Nicholsons had owned a gray Volkswagen was not unlike the thought processes of people who said to him from time to time, "Oh, you live in New York? Maybe you know my cousin."

On the other hand, there *had* been a gray Volkswagen, and except for a freakish forewarning from her adolescence Lydia might not have come home from the beach. With what to explain it to the police? Something fairly common on the modern scene, like interrupted drug traffic of some kind?

Desmond had reached the Chilton house, and he was too late: the big car was gone and there was an unmistakable and final silence about the place. *Silence.* Lack of sound. The oddity which Mrs. Tadlock's rampaging in her kitchen had driven from his mind was Lydia's answer to his question about Hatch's arrival ". . . yes, I see him outside."

"See" wasn't the operative word where a motorcycle was concerned. Desmond wheeled his car.

Lydia was not really nervous about the unlocked dining-room window; she put it down, like the cream-colored sash at the foot of the enclosed staircase, to an accident of the pre-wedding entertaining. Smoke, perfume, flowers, the simple body heat generated by numbers of people: someone had wanted to let in some fresh air.

Still, she was glad she hadn't known about that very accessible window when she had gone downstairs in the small hours to examine the bolt on the cellar door, and for some atavistic reason she put off her packing. Upstairs, she was careful not to say to herself, it was possible to be cornered.

The episode at the beach had left her queerly unsure of herself; it was as if in some way her judgment had become impaired. She even thought as she hung up after talking to Desmond that his definition of a "kid" was like a reference to bellboys, with no actual age involved. Certainly the stocky compact figure with the lawn rake had none of the still-sprouting look of youth.

The telephone rang again under her hand, and in her new incertitude she jiggled the receiver in the act of lifting it. It was Candide, who surprisingly did not want baby-sitting or other services but had called to say good-bye. She sounded enormously pleased with herself. "Do you know that you were actually right about Harrison? He's been hanging about like this waiting for friends who may want to buy the house, and apparently he thought—trust Harrison—that it would be intrusive to broach the matter right away. So it's all working out very well."

She really did say that, thought Lydia. She said neutrally, "Well, good."

"Of course, it was a tragedy about Mother," said Candide, catching up late, "and Jones feels it too. It's been much too harrowing to discuss, as I know you understand. He is pleased, though, now that we know about Harrison. Some of those North Shore people are absolutely Victorian. Well, good-bye, Lydia," she said, back in full patronizing stride. "Do you know, I have a notion that Desmond Moran is interested, and you could actually do worse. You must be, let's see—"

"Three years younger than you are. If you have a

pencil and a long sheet of paper it's fairly easy to work out," said Lydia. "Give my best to Harry . . ."

So much for the pea jacket and the sneakers, she thought presently. Jones Haviland, free soul extraordinary, had prudently not wanted to jeopardize any lucrative commissions over the custody battle for a child, and if Desmond was right about the money involved, it would have been publicized.

And: do worse than Desmond Moran, indeed. For the moment, Candide's pseudo-endorsement loomed as a great black mark against him, but it could not quite obliterate a tingle of awareness. He had suggested dinner at his apartment, if she were still feeling shaken-up, so Lydia supposed that she must soon ease her surprisingly sore shoulder and knee into something more suitable than a robe. Darkness wasn't far off, there was a sprinkle of rain like flung salt against the windows, the yard boy—man?—was heading briskly for the house.

Emmett Blake, emerging from the post office just before it closed, was unaware of the rain. He had collected an electric light bill and a single letter addressed to Mr. and Mrs. Emmett Blake in a cramped and difficult hand. The Boston postmark was clear, but it had taken him moments to decipher, and attach a memory to, the name above the familiar address in the upper left-hand corner.

J. Harney.

Chapter 17

The superintendent of the Boston apartment building was a man of few words, as his handwriting indicated, but only a few were necessary. He had written: "You folks been good to me and you should know that a man named Moran has been snooping around about you and your friends the Nicholsons. Yours very truly, J. Harney."

Paula Blake wasted very little time in astonishment over an entirely unlooked-for development. Typically, her mind was already as busy as an oyster with an introduced grain of sand. The smoke from the cigarette she had lit from the end of the previous one did not waver. "Who do you suppose Desmond Moran has told about his snoopings?"

"My guess would be nobody, yet," said Emmett. "He's a newspaperman, he'd hardly go out on a limb."

"He'd certainly be alive to the laws of libel." Paula's green glance turned brooding. "No use dwelling on it, but we haven't seen the woods for the trees. The day you saw Lydia getting into his car—"

"*Might* have seen," Emmett corrected. "I was in the middle of a left turn at the time and she was wearing a scarf. And that note on her door certainly wasn't addressed to anyone."

"Even so. Oh, don't think I'm criticizing. *I* thought this afternoon that he was lining himself up to be Candide Blackwood's next husband, and trying to get chummy with the little boy. But"—a nod of Paula's head indicated the room on the other side of the tiny hall—"we should have known. If you think about it, Lydia Peel isn't the type to sneak into other people's houses. While you're thinking about it, you might make us another drink."

They had lit a fire against the rainy dark afternoon, and gold chased itself occasionally around the curve of a doorknob and over the grain of polished wood. In the kitchen, Emmett whistled his familiar notes, and when he came back and put an icy glass in her hand, Paula said sharply, "You're going to have to stop that, you know. You were doing it when Desmond Moran was here this afternoon, and I had to shout. Now, who would he have talked to in Boston besides Harney?"

Emmett considered. "The Morrows, I suppose. But as our departed friend would have said, not to worry. They're—"

He stopped short. Paula said musingly, "No, they're not quite harmless. Remember Thanksgiving, when it was so windy and dirty out and we were down on our hands and knees in the lobby and it was Mrs. Morrow who found the contact lens? Beside which, I'd swear that she was on hand for the delivery of that presentation stuff."

Emmett did not have to answer. There was a small but deep silence, laced together by intricate and dovetailing thoughts. Paula, poking at an ice cube with her forefinger, broke the silence. "You having been in charge of this department, how, er, good would you say we'd been to Harney?"

Emmett smiled slightly. "As to possible repercussion? Good enough," he said.

". . . All right now? Damn that Hatch!" said Desmond, forcefully and unfairly.

He had arrived at the Donahue house to find a total stranger, a stocky man with graying dark hair, rapping imperatively on the front living-room window; he turned out to be an unemployed uncle pressed into service by Hatch when his motorcycle had broken down, and with a bad cold he had no intention of staying out in the rain. In Lydia's state of mind he had been the man from the beach, lulling her with the lawn rake, determined to break into the house.

"I'm fine. I'm sorry. I mean, I'm not usually like this," said Lydia, very busy with a cigarette. Because she supposed she had looked to be in distress, as the phrase went, Desmond had put his arms around her and then he had kissed her anxiously. She was not sure where they went from here—perhaps he had kissed her and she had responded out of pure mountain-climbing rationale—and she felt a need to put words, any kind of words, between them. "I do live in a house in Santa Fe, all by myself, and I honestly don't faint or carry on when there's a new mailman or meter reader."

"I'm sure you don't," said Desmond, and he was as distracted as she; having lit a cigarette of his own, he placed it carefully in an ash tray and lit another. "But I can't have anything happening to you. What would I say to the Donahues?" He had wandered to a window. He said, "Believe it or not, this is the police."

Lydia, who had never had so much as a parking ticket in her life, had always been daunted by policemen. She marveled at as well as deplored people who openly hurled imprecations at them and even, if newspaper accounts could be believed, sometimes bit them while being taken rightfully into custody. This feeling underwent a sharp change within the next few minutes.

The experienced glance that shot from her to Desmond? The study of the third and orphan cigarette? Whatever it was, Lydia was aware of being assessed as a female who had gone to the beach in search of adventure which had gotten out of hand. She was very conscious of her robe, which she had not had time to change, and the fact that she was dealing with a man who would never go to a beach unless in swimming trunks when it was ninety in the shade did not help. The mewing sounds echoed in her own ears as ridiculous in the telling, and she sat up straighter with surprise when the sergeant said, "Well, there was no cat there when we checked the place out. Completely deserted. What we did find—"

The telephone began to ring; Lydia ignored it.

"—was a candle stub and a burned spoon." On the couch beside her Desmond gave a small stir, almost of recognition. "Could be a junkie, I suppose."

"But more probably," said Lydia, driven to her feet by the continuing peal of the telephone, furious at the cold glance that had swept from her face to her sandaled bare feet, "someone who had dropped in to make some brown gravy, it always comes out best in bathhouses for some reason, and was caramelizing sugar."

She closed the living-room door audibly behind her, a gesture she normally equated, in terms of mannerliness, with a sharp kick in the shins. When she answered the telephone it must have been with a carried-over crispness, because Paula Blake said at once, "I've taken you away from your packing, I can tell."

Lydia assured her that she had not; any further explanation seemed involved and pointless.

"I have to burble to somebody," said Paula, and indeed she sounded strung-up and gay. "Emmett got a letter today from a New York gallery—the man in charge is a friend of friends—and one of the artists for a show has fallen through because his wife just committed suicide or has just been committed, I'm not clear which, and Emmett's work just might fit in. The letter got here a day late and it certainly wouldn't do at this point to be looking blasé, so we're at the station now. Isn't it marvelous, if it comes off, and will you tell Susan?"

Lydia said yes on both counts, because surely Susan and Santa Fe still had a very real existence? Because of the time difference, she had a weird, shutter-action image of sun-flushed, branch-patterned adobe superimposed on the wet black windows.

". . . suppose it's an extravagance for me to go too," Paula was saying in her ear, "but I'm feeling a bit mossy and rural and I'd like a look at the bright lights and the muggers. I hope you're doing something nice on this ghastly evening."

"I'm going out to dinner in a while." As once before, something close to superstition kept Lydia from mentioning Desmond's name, although Paula appeared to have no notion that her house had been entered that afternoon, and she dismissed at once her own impression of an inviting little pause. Susan's sister wasn't coy.

"Well, enjoy," said Paula, a locution at once airy, ungrammatical and somehow doubtful, "and wish us luck, and God bless."

It had no ring of blasphemy. In the living room, Lydia

discovered that the policeman had departed, leaving behind him the kind of silence that suggested a few sharp exchanges. Desmond, who had left this number for his photographer friend, was gazing at her expectantly. She said, "That was Paula Blake," and explained.

It crossed her mind as she spoke that even twenty-four hours ago she would have delivered this intelligence with a certain amount of satisfaction. Now she was only aware that Desmond had received it with astonishing interest. Because it had upset his theories? His gaze on hers was speculative and unseeing. Lydia said, "I'm going to get dressed," doubted if he had even heard her, and went upstairs.

When she came down again, there were drinks waiting in the living room, which did not seem in the least odd although technically she was the hostess here, and Desmond was at the telephone. Lydia, passing him on her way to the kitchen for pretzel sticks and sharp mustard, paused involuntarily at the sound coming through the receiver which he held a little away from his ear: it had the ferocious edge of broken glass. Desmond tried unsuccessful interruptions—"That's too . . . If I could just . . ."—and played absently with an end of the sash slung over the latch of the stairway door. Released, it cast a shadow like a swaying black snake.

He finally managed to give a number which Lydia recognized as his own. He said when he hung up, "That was Mrs. Tadlock. The stupid chickens have been sent to bed without their food or water or whatever they're due for because Tadlock's been stuck in Elder with a broken-down truck and she doesn't believe a word of it, at the top of her lungs. She may have had a nip of her own wine. Tadlock's the photographer," he explained to Lydia's bewildered face. "I left my number for after seven o'clock, if that's all right with you, because I think your film might be interesting . . ."

The telephone rang while they were still standing beside it, as though an infuriated Mrs. Tadlock had somehow managed to overhear him. It was first Tom and then Nancy Donahue in Florida; they were taking a later flight back than they had planned, and as they would miss Lydia, they seemed inclined to chat. Desmond brought Lydia her drink and a cigarette and an ash tray, for which she thanked him with a smile that froze and then disappeared.

"I forgot all about Nancy's birthday begonia," she said, hanging up and heading distractedly for the double doors in the living room. "I was supposed to water it and have little chats with it and now it's probably—"

It was. "Buy another one," suggested Desmond, "and if you have to get a different color, tell her it was transformed with rage when she left it."

But his manner had changed subtly, Lydia thought; while he did not actually hurry her through her drink, he prowled so restively about with his own that she put down her glass without finishing it, went through her now familiar routine with the lights, got her coat.

The rain had stopped, but in the way that a bell has stopped being rung; echoes of it still shook through the night. Lydia tried to memorize and tuck away for herself the compound of soaked earth, wet bark and moss, a trace of salt. Occasionally the headlights picked up new leaves like green fireflies, and Desmond took corners with care.

"Glissant lorsque humide," she said out of an irrelevant memory, and caught the edge of an abstracted smile. "France or Canada?"

"Canada. It seems like something much more exotic

than 'Slippery when wet.' "

She had been so bemused by the drenched quality of the air, a condition for which Indians did ritual dances in New Mexico, that the Elder's Farms station, which was not on the way to Desmond's apartment, came as a surprise. The train Paula Blake had announced was a popular one, and there were a number of cars parked along the platform—among them, as Desmond cruised slowly by, the dark green Austin.

"You thought that was a tale about going to New York," said Lydia. She wasn't defensive—that was far behind her—but genuinely curious. "Why would they have bothered? What would be the point?"

"Misdirection," said Desmond briefly, "in case they were leaving, but to points west or north. Or because they wanted you to be convinced that they were not on the scene tonight." He was flicking an occasional glance at the rear-view mirror as he drove. "Were the Blakes ever in the house?"

It was a casual question. It was also peculiarly chilling, like a doctor asking with professional calm if she had been in contact with someone harboring a fatal disease. "Yes, once," said Lydia. His meaning was inescapable; he was thinking of the unlocked dining-room window. "But—"

They didn't have a chance to fiddle with anything, she had been about to say, but realized that that wasn't necessarily the case. The Blakes had admired the house, exclaimed over the size of the fireplace and the Dutch oven beside it, been struck by the old black range in the kitchen, but certainly they had not been with her every moment while she poured brandy.

She thought with sudden cold of that unlocked window—and of the alien sash on the enclosed stairway, and the icy air at the back of the house on the night the Graces came. The Blakes would have had the back door mapped. She thought of the clock-radio which had toppled in the corner bedroom as though someone brushing hastily against it had altered its balance so that the tiniest of vibrations, even a tremor of wind, had upset it. She had been reassured at the pristine state of the lock on the closet door, but of course damage to that would have had to come later, once the wedding-present cache had been located. So that if something happened to her it would appear that she had interrupted and been foolish enough to try to stop a burglar after all the silver?

A moment of actual dizziness possessed Lydia; she had to press herself back against the seat, hard. "You think they were at the beach today." There had been only one person in the bathhouse, she was sure of it, but in a terrifying sense one was *they;* each carried the characteristics of the other about with him as indelibly as his own fingerprints. She had thought of their relationship in terms of solidarity, but conspiracy was infinitely more binding. "And you expected the candle and the spoon."

"Very classic," said Desmond. "Very portable. And nobody came out in the open to chase you, which somebody all that strung-out would have done. There had to be an opportunity for another try."

To kill me, said Lydia to herself. *To kill me.* "A body identified as that of Lydia Peel . . ." No, that was when the police had only your teeth to go by, and at the beach there had been the Volvo with her handbag in it. The beach, a pure gift with her note left on the door, the note unpinned and placed far from the house but retrievable in case anything went wrong, as it had, so that Lydia would not remark later on the strangeness of its disappearance.

To see the note at all, Emmett or Paula or both had driven to the house this afternoon to—carry out the robbery-and-murder scene by broad daylight? Or carry her off in their car on some pretext? It was true that Lydia had turned them over in her mind, in an academic way, as faces Mrs. Chilton might have seen just before she died, but if Emmett had come alone and said that Paula had received some frightful message about Susan and was in a state of collapse, she would have gone with him unquestioningly.

Her acceptance of all this was not really astonishing; it was as though some inefficient sentry in her brain had been observing from the first and simply not bothered to report until now. What was astonishing was:

"Why?" asked Lydia suddenly, with the deep instinctive anger of someone under the ultimate threat. "I scarcely know the Blakes. What have I done to them, apart from bringing them a mirror?"

And Desmond told her.

Chapter 18

The long grass on the hill behind the apartment was so wet that it was as much of an uphill wade as a climb. Desmond did not use his flashlight in spite of the almost total darkness and an occasional near-graze with a hickory tree; something that he could not identify was bothering him.

It was not the fact that he had found the back door of the apartment unlocked. That was standard practice with him, as he had never gotten around to having a duplicate made of the key which Mrs. Chilton had warned him was the only one in existence, and the apartment windows would mean a wriggling squeeze. A thief would have given a pitying laugh at his typewriter, and the photograph he had removed from Emmett Blake's bureau drawer never left his wallet. Still —unobtrusively, because Lydia looked shaken enough as it was—he had made sure that the closets and the shower were untenanted before departing on his brief, essential errand.

Nor was it the fact of Lydia's presence in the now locked and lighted apartment. Danger for her lay in the Donahue house, where a different pattern of lamps and the Volvo parked in the driveway would announce her to be, if not now, because she had told Paula Blake that she was going out to dinner, at some point later this evening. In spite of this camouflage he had, superstitiously, led her around to the front door of the apartment, which faced the brook and the hill.

. . . Below him, the Blake house was dark, which was no guarantee whatever of its being empty. Two could play at that game, reflected Desmond, and no hair stirred on the back of his neck at all.

He went quietly through the orchard and, guided by the just-visible line of the low stone wall, angled sharply to his left. He crossed the wall at a point which brought him out on the far side of the garage, an addition to the house and padlocked as he had expected. Fortunately the driveway wasn't graveled, and the wet ground drank up his footsteps without sound. He returned to the window he had hoped and trusted would be there, and beamed the flashlight in.

Upended wheelbarrow against the far wall—hard to imagine Blake trundling one—and, in the corner, a collection of garden tools. The shovel had dried earth clinging to it. In the center of the cement floor, a paler space too short and too narrow to have been occupied by the Austin, which Lydia had seen parked outside in any case on both of her visits. A Volkswagen would have fitted into it—and at the back of the space was an oil stain. No, it was more than that; when Desmond stepped a little to the side and moved the flashlight beam, it was identifiably fresh oil.

The dark house beyond the garage did not seem to be holding its breath. Where was it now, the Nicholsons' old gray Volkswagen, and what was the nagging worry that had pursued him up the hill . . . ?

* * *

In Desmond's apartment, Lydia had steeled herself for a possible eruption from the telephone, which would be the photographer, Tadlock; otherwise, she thought, her nervous heart would give one huge and final thump.

How dense she had been, looking back. No law said that you had to like or be at ease with the sister of a good friend, but from the very beginning, from Emmett's overheard fury when she had arrived on the doorstep with the mirror, something had been wrong —the lack, perhaps, of the spark generated between people by mutual knowledge and affection for a third.

The envelope addressed to the Bureau of Vital Statistics in Philadelphia: it would have seemed wise to them to discover Susan's birth date when a birthday present for her sister had just been delivered, and a letter apparently signed by Susan and enclosing the proper fee would give them their answer.

Paula, blind-as-a-bat Paula, looking up a telephone number without glasses when Lydia drove by the gas station; that accounted for her altered appearance. Glasses must be an encumbrance when you didn't need them. Lydia, in her steadying halt after the flight from the beach, had stared at the campaign poster of a woman candidate adorned with glasses and a beard, and hadn't made the connection even then.

The continuing correspondence between Elder's Farms and Santa Fe, based on old letters from Susan, and Susan sensing some alteration: "Something tells me she isn't finding life in the country all it's cracked up to be."

But Susan never flew; nothing would coax her onto a jet.

The calm, the frightful calm with which they had

watched Mrs. Chilton drop sparks on her tweed skirt. Because Mrs. Chilton, pursuing her newest hobby, wanted to dig in the old foundation as Simon Wister had told her she could, and if she dug deep enough, she would find—

Lydia's feet had now carried her into Desmond's kitchen, which, converted from a darkroom, had very commodious sinks. She opened the refrigerator distractedly and looked in at Port Salut, a T-bone steak, mushrooms in a plastic bag, cans of beer, tomatoes which he must have been ripening for a long time because they were actually red. The steak was evidently for their dinner, and she turned on the oven broiler, experimentally, found a colander and washed the lettuce.

There was a faint and distant sound of thunder—puzzling, because to the east a great swath of sky had been scraped clear of clouds and there were stars, not the poked-through jewels of the Southwest but a remote scatter. Lydia wandered back into the living room, wished sharply that Desmond would come back, looked at his covered typewriter—he was tidier about this than he was with coats—and, after a very short argument with her conscience, lifted off the cover.

She supposed that looking at a writer's work uninvited was tantamount to exploring a diary. But any aspect of Desmond had become fresh and valuable to her, and not in any prying sense; it was a little like, for gift purposes, wanting to know the size of his gloves or his socks.

The page in the typewriter was numbered 206, and it read: "stead of Holt replying, he turned his back. She wasn't surprised. Welles Roland killed Mrs. Chilton."

Lydia put the cover back on the typewriter as though

she had found some unspeakable prose. Her fingers shook. It went wildly through her mind that no wonder Holt had turned his back without replying; he had been as thunderstruck as she.

Desmond had survived a plane crash in which most of the other passengers had burned to death, and Mrs. Chilton had died by fire. He had liked Mrs. Chilton, he had failed in his attempt to rescue her, he was here in Elder's Farms on sick leave . . .

A mocking melody had begun to arrange itself in her head. Six notes, idle, not very loud, some comforting old refrain. "Keep the home fires burning . . ."

It wasn't in her head. There was someone outside in the night that still dripped and rustled. Desmond, back so soon, choosing this of all songs to announce his arrival?

"Keep the ho—" The whistling stopped short, but Lydia had had time to estimate its direction. It wasn't coming from the hill but along the driveway that continued past the Chilton house, and now it was followed by another and closer sound, the shattering of glass. The noise was so immediate and elemental that Lydia seemed to feel it in her throat, catching and hurting her breath. She flattened her palms wildly against her cheeks, and took them away because the telephone was ringing.

The voice at the other end of the line said in a nasal and leisurely fashion, "Hey, Desmond Moran there?"

"Mr. Tadlock? Would you hang up right away and call the—"

"Ain't a damn thing on that film. Exposed, all of it."

"Send the police to Mrs. Chilton's. Hurry!" cried Lydia into the telephone, because she had nerved herself to twitch a drawn curtain aside and the crash of glass was the windshield of Desmond's car being battered with a rock by Emmett Blake. She couldn't see his other hand, but she knew that a man could be expected to rush out and investigate that sound at once. *Welles Roland* had found an echo in her stunned brain: that, or something very much like it, was the name Desmond had said he had used to lure the Blakes out of their house, and they were turning it against him. There could be only one purpose for that. They had infiltrated here, they had him targeted, and he didn't even suspect it.

And Emmett had seen her, around that twitch of curtain. His surprise communicated itself like an earth tremor, and then he was running toward the apartment. He still held the rock, and Lydia still couldn't see his other hand. To be trapped, to be beaten back into a closet— She heard the telephone receiver miss its cradle and roll and hit the floor while she was running for the other door and plummeting out into the dark.

To light-blinded eyes, the blackness was absolute. Lydia stumbled almost immediately over some tough low-growing bush, felt her scraped knee falter, was pulled steadyingly upright. She said on an urgent gasp, "*Desmond,*" before her wits informed her that she had not been so much pulled as wrenched, that this fierce grip belonged to a woman, that these people hunted in pairs, like mambas.

"Here she is," called Paula quietly, and Emmett arrived with the gun.

Inside the apartment, Emmett said sharply to Lydia, "Where's Moran?"

Lydia stared at him with silent hatred, although it was Paula who had blocked her twisting attempt at escape by slamming her hard against the apartment wall. She was very strong. The back of Lydia's head hurt and she thought she could feel blood, but by holding Emmett's gaze, and by connection Paula's, she might keep them from noticing the receiverless telephone in shadow under a window. Had Tadlock paid any attention to that frantic request? Would the police pay any attention?

Paula moved angrily. *"He asked you—"*

"He's gone to a photographer he knows, to pick up my film," said Lydia, fast. Every second counted. "He thinks it's going to be blank, and that's going to look very sus—"

"Listen," said Paula, and the thin high whine of a telephone receiver off its hook, covered until now by voices and tension, seemed to swell into the room. The Blakes looked at the telephone, at Lydia, at each other. Change of plan: it quivered on the air like the after-image of a flashbulb.

". . . I'll get the car," said Paula, and she ran.

The key, the reciprocal key to the Chilton house which the Blakes had found and used on the night they killed Mrs. Chilton. Desmond had thought of it that afternoon as he approached their house, and then had it driven from his mind by the attack on Lydia at the beach. Or not quite: some buried awareness that sound carried after rain had made him engage the car door on his side very gently when they arrived at the apartment, so that a listener would have heard only a single slam.

But a watcher looking out of a dark house might have been able to see two occupants in the car as it went by. Lydia wouldn't have been identifiable, Desmond reminded himself—he was using his flashlight to get back through the orchard, queerly sure that the house behind him had been empty all along—but his mind presented him suddenly with a memory of the Austin in town on the snowy day when he had given Lydia a lift. He was always interested in that particular car, and it seemed to him now that Emmett Blake had glanced back with a similar interest in his.

The telephone call from Paula Blake, with the gratuitous information that they were about to take a train for New York, could be regarded as a decoy: "Come and investigate all you like, it's perfectly safe." But they would hardly expect Lydia to arm herself with pick and shovel and lantern. They had seen her with Desmond at least once, and they would certainly remember that he had been there at the old foundation while Harry danced with rage beside him.

Was it possible that by bringing Lydia to his apartment, and leaving her there alone while he tied the Nicholsons' Volkswagen to the Blakes, he had placed her in a trap?

Common sense said that the doors were locked. His nerves observed that where killers were concerned, killers who knew their quarry to be inside, locked doors and windows of a nuisance size for getting through were not an insuperable obstacle.

Desmond topped the hill, breathing hard—and after the racing thoughts that had verged on the frantic the apartment below him was tranquil. No shadows wrestled across its curtained windows, and the only sounds in the night were a distant tremble of thunder and the tiny, busy aftermath of the rain.

Not thunder, he realized. The new roll-down doors of Mrs. Chilton's garage, of which she had been very proud although she said their rumbling ought to herald a new Cadillac at least instead of her ancient vehicle. And here came the Volkswagen, its bright lights dazzling and blinding, heading for the apartment. Desmond plunged down the hill.

Chapter 19

The slender single apartment key eluded him in his jolting run, like any necessary object in a necessitous moment, but his car keys, tagged, bulkier, came readily into his hand. Even better? The Volkswagen, padlocked into the garage, ostensibly unconnected with the Blakes, who used the dark green Austin on their infrequent trips into the town, must be an escape hatch as well as their murder transport. If he could keep it from reaching the apartment at all—

It was instinct rather than ordered thought. Desmond rounded the corner of the apartment, did not even check at the astonishing sight of his demolished windshield, and was still too late: although the driveway was a long one—he had cursed it often enough in the February snow—the Volkswagen was glittering down on him less than twenty-five feet away. He could see as well as hear its acceleration when he stepped into its beams—and he could hear something else which the closed windows and noisy motor might have been drowning for the car's occupants: the sound of a siren.

At the last possible second he threw the flashlight with all his strength at the driver's side of the windshield. The headlights swung in a wild, uncontrolled arc. The Volkswagen left the driveway, careened over rough ground, wrenched to avoid a tree, returned to the driveway in time to collide with the police cruiser, siren now off, proceeding down it.

And Desmond, who had jumped into the glassy interior of his own car with the intention of giving chase, could now see what the blinding headlights had hidden from him before. There was only one person in the Volkswagen, and it was Paula Blake. He said aloud, "God in heaven," and ran for the apartment.

He paid no attention to Emmett Blake who, peculiarly, paid no attention to him either but walked out the door to meet the policeman. He went directly to Lydia, in a chair with the rigid, arms-gripping attitude of someone about to be electrocuted. It seemed ludicrous to ask, "Are you all right?" but he had to hear her speak, had to assure himself that she wasn't in shock.

"Yes," said Lydia, and her voice was her own although she was extremely pale. "Desmond, look at the page in your typewriter."

Emmett Blake hadn't closed the door behind him, and voices came fragmentarily in: ". . . going on here?" ". . . out for a walk, I'm an artist, Officer, and I'd been working, and heard someone screaming for help . . . don't know whether there's been some kind of party or what, but the young lady may have been drinking . . ."

Desmond listened to that and smiled at Lydia simply because he wanted to coax a response from her. He lifted off his typewriter cover, studied the few lines on the page in it, said thoughtfully, "I think I'll leave that right there. There must be fingerprints, which, not being dead as hoped, I'm in a position to—"

He broke off as the door swung wide and the police

sergeant, looking grim because the cruiser was a new one and its left front fender was now buckled, shepherded the Blakes in. He was the same officer who had been at the Donahues' earlier, and his eyes widened and then narrowed at the sight of Lydia. He said, "This gentleman tells me—"

"He's a liar," said Lydia, brief and clear. "He had a gun, he threw it outside somewhere, and he knows perfectly well what's the matter with me." She took her head away from the chairback, and left a smear of blood behind. "When his wife left to get the Volkswagen, I pretended to lose consciousness, and he felt the back of my head to see if I was shamming. Look at his fingers, look at his handkerchief—"

The traces of blood, the recovered gun, the Volkswagen's registration in the name of Naomi R. Nicholson—the pair they were still calling the Blakes insisted that it was being kept for friends temporarily in the Southwest—were enough to warrant an investigation of the foundation. In the meantime, both were charged with aggravated assault and Paula, in what seemed the ultimate in irony, with reckless driving.

Pending the outcome of the digging, the photograph of Paula Blake which Desmond had removed from the bureau drawer was sent to Susan in Santa Fe. She telephoned at once to say that it was not her sister. She had not been out of the city over the weekend at all; that had apparently been a ruse to keep Lydia from calling about any puzzling oddities. She said in a stunned voice, "But I had a letter from Paula just a couple of weeks ago," and was told that a number of her own letters, certainly enough to provide a groundwork for correspondence, had been discovered. Even then she was incredulous. "Both of them . . . *no*—"

She was quite right, and Desmond had been half-wrong. The bodies exhumed from their charred, impromptu, debris-filled grave proved to be those of Philip Nicholson and Paula Blake.

The dispatch of spouses who refused to divorce, by means of the gun which was ultimately traced as having been given to Philip Nicholson in partial payment of a debt, certainly wasn't new, but few people could have fallen into as tailor-made a situation as Emmett Blake. It was even possible to speculate that if he had not become heir to his cousin's property his wife, and Naomi Nicholson's husband, might still have been alive.

In Blake's case, divorce was not even particularly desirable; Paula received the regular dividend checks which provided the frills in their marriage. Naomi Nicholson was not so patient. She had married out of boredom and a realization of the passing years, and when as Paula's secretary at the advertising agency she had inevitably met Emmett, the mutual attraction was instant. Her husband's few days on the hospital's critical list in November might have started her thinking.

Even then, if it had not been a warm Christmas . . . but Paula had been impetuous about taking early possession of the Elder's Farms house, and Emmett Blake had instantly let Naomi know. Philip Nicholson, still so infatuated with his wife that he traveled with her photograph, also dealt in antiques on the side. (In New Orleans he had given a worthless check for an old music box.) It would have been a simple matter for Naomi to persuade him that a trip to Elder's Farms, ahead of the Blakes, as he thought, would be worth his while. "They can't know what's there; they wouldn't miss a few things."

"And they knew they were safe from Susan, as long as the correspondence kept up," said Lydia. They were in Desmond's apartment, briefly a place of terror, because she had had to stay in Elder's Farms to testify to the assault. She had been introduced to the nutshells.

Desmond nodded. "And Naomi must have told a few people they were moving to the Southwest for her husband's health—that's why those snapshots of her in light winter clothing in case it seemed wise to dispatch one."

Lydia had seen the snapshot. The cream pullover was the one the woman she still thought of as Paula Blake had been wearing the afternoon she opened the door and said "You must be Lydia Peel."

"She wears colored contact lenses, I suppose. I knew Paula had green eyes, from Susan."

"Yes. I saw the container in her desk and like a fool I didn't recognize it. Everybody in my family has very good eyes," said Desmond, gazing with bland inquiry at Lydia.

"Good for them, it must be a source of happiness to you all," said Lydia, matching him. "Why did she bother, coming to a town where nobody had met Paula Blake?"

Desmond shrugged. "I suppose it would be an elementary precaution to look as much as possible like the woman you were supplanting. Particularly with such a noticeable feature. She got the contact lenses in Boston, just in case, I imagine—it would be a risk in a small place like Elder's Farms, and they take getting used to. I called Mrs. Morrow—I thought she deserved to know what my descent on them was all about—and she said she helped find one of the lenses in the lobby one day, and Blake picked it up before she could, but she had thought it was green. The other thing they'd neglected to tell me was that on the one occasion when they'd met the Nicholsons, Mrs. Nicholson was carrying some kind of dispatch case, and they had the impression that it was a business as well as a social visit."

". . . And they almost got away with it," said Lydia wonderingly.

"No reason why they shouldn't," said Desmond, practical, "except for Mrs. Chilton, and nobody could have expected a digging enthusiast who had gotten permission from Wister and wasn't going to give up. And then you arrived on the scene, and that would still have been all right if you hadn't seen Naomi without her glasses. My guess is"—Emmett Blake and Naomi Nicholson had acquired lawyers, and were adamantly saying nothing—"that they thought you had taken the snapshot and then somehow they found out it was me."

It had been a mistake to mention Mrs. Chilton; Lydia's vivid gaze had turned sober.

"Wait," said Desmond imperatively. He departed for his car, whose windshield he had not gotten around to doing anything about, came back with a bottle of wine, uncorked it, got two glasses. "This stuff is terrible beyond belief," he said, "but under the circumstances we might drink a very careful toast to the Tadlocks. Slainte."

Lydia knew that it was only an Irish toast; something about the steadied meeting of their eyes made it much more. She lifted her glass, felt a fleeting compassion for Susan, who was going to have to discover all there was to discover about Miles Marsh, thought rebelliously that nothing and no one was going to spoil this. She said, "Slainte."

THE END